Shaun Murphy's
steering wheel o
toward the

Suddenly, beams of blinding brightness arched across his path. He hit the brakes. The beams swung to one side and the red compact car careened off the road and plowed into some bushes.

Shaun climbed out and jogged to where the car had come to rest.

"I'm really sorry," he called. "Are you okay?"

"Door's stuck." The driver's voice was muted by the closed vehicle. Shaun gave the handle a jerk and it opened. The driver swiveled in the seat and looked up at him. He gaped. There, in all her glory, was Delia Blanchard, the woman who had heartlessly abandoned him on their wedding night twelve years ago without so much as a word—or even a goodbye note.

* * *

VALERIE HANSEN

was thirty when she awoke to the presence of the Lord in her life and turned to Jesus. In the years that followed she worked with young children, both in church and secular environments, as well as raised a family of her own and played foster mother to a wide assortment of furred and feathered critters.

Married to her high school sweetheart since age seventeen, she now lives in an old farmhouse she and her husband renovated with their own hands. She loves to hike the wooded hills behind the house and reflect on the marvelous turn her life has taken. Not only is she privileged to reside among the loving, accepting folks in the breathtakingly beautiful Ozark mountains of Arkansas, she also gets to share her personal faith by telling the stories of her heart for the Love Inspired line.

Life doesn't get much better than that!

VALERIE HANSEN

Deadly Payoff

Steeple
Hill®

Published by Steeple Hill Books™

Special thanks and acknowledgment
to Valerie Hansen for her contribution to
THE SECRETS OF STONELEY miniseries

STEEPLE HILL BOOKS

Steeple
Hill®

ISBN-13: 978-0-373-44242-3
ISBN-10:   0-373-44242-4

DEADLY PAYOFF

www.SteepleHill.com

Printed in U.S.A.

They that trust in their wealth, and boast themselves
in the multitude of their riches;
none of them can by any means redeem his brother,
nor give to God a ransom for him.
—*Psalms* 49:6–7

This is a series about six sisters. I only had one.

That was plenty! I kept telling Mom and Dad I wanted a brother, but would they listen to me? No!

So this book is for Audrey. Nah-nah-nah-nah-nah!

ONE

Leaving her life in Hawaii and flying to Eastern Maine so often, even for the sake of her family, was beginning to wear on Delia Blanchard. All she really wanted to do was stand on the warm sands of Oahu, breathe deeply of the sweet tropical air and feel its balmy breezes on her face. Instead, here she was, back on the Atlantic coast again and stuck within the cold, stone walls of the Blanchard mansion. It was enough to make any wahine shiver, even a transplanted one like her.

She fluffed her short, dark hair, forced a smile and aimed it especially at her youngest sister, Juliet. "You okay, honey?"

Juliet nodded. "Fine. I'm glad you came."

"How could I refuse when my family needed me?"

"We do. I wish you could stay longer this time."

"I should have come when you were in the hospital," Delia said, giving her a warm, sisterly hug, "but by the time I got word and was able to book a flight back to the mainland, you were out of danger."

"I understand." Juliet smiled. "Besides, I'd rather see you when I'm not flat on my back in some depressing hospital."

Delia wasn't about to pursue this line of conversation. The sisters had enough problems without rehashing Juliet's deliberate poisoning, not to mention Portia's foiled kidnapping and Rissa's brush with death on the cliffs a few weeks ago.

Her brown eyes narrowed as she took in the darkly paneled walls and the sweeping walnut staircase with its heavy, ornate balustrades. "Speaking of depressing… This place gives me the worst shivers every time I come back. I know you'll be glad to marry Brandon and move out of here."

"It's not so bad. I suppose you would notice the contrast more than the rest of us," the blond young woman said. "There's a big difference between the Maine coast and the shores of Oahu."

"*That's* an understatement."

The heavy front door swung open to admit a gust of icy wind and three more of Delia's sisters. Twins Portia and Rissa led and Bianca followed. "Sorry we're late. Father insisted on taking the scenic route in spite of the bad weather."

Delia laughed. "You should have ridden with Miranda and Aunt Winnie or Juliet and me. My rental car may not be as luxurious as Father's town car but we got back here a lot faster." She wrapped her arms close around herself, chilled despite her

long-sleeved, belted sweater, and squelched a
shudder as her sisters shed their coats. "I don't know
why Father insisted we visit the cemetery again. I
think births and happy occasions like that should be
celebrated, not anniversaries of loss."

The others murmured agreement, growing more
subdued the moment their father, Ronald Blanchard,
joined them. Tall and broad shouldered, with attrac-
tive streaks of gray at his temples, he cut a dashing
figure. Although he was in his late fifties, he still
drew a lot of attention from the female residents of
Stoneley, Maine. His overall countenance, however,
left a lot to be desired. Delia couldn't help compar-
ing it with the brewing, New England storm.
Happily, the gray clouds outside would soon lift
while her father seemed to be growing more morose
by the minute. Anyone who wasn't aware of his
decades-long estrangement from his recently
deceased wife, Trudy, might think that he had
actually cared for her.

The sisters knew better, of course. They had
grown up in a home where the mere mention of their
mother's name was strictly forbidden. Ronald Blanchard, like his own father, Howard, was a hard, un-
forgiving man. Whatever he said, went, and no one
dared question his edicts. No one except *her*.

Thoughtful, Delia pressed her lips together.
Perhaps she had inherited more negative family traits
than she liked to admit. She'd tried for twelve years
to forgive her father for having had her marriage
annulled and she still harbored a grudge. Yes, she'd

been underage at the time. And, yes, she'd gone against his wishes. But that didn't mean it couldn't have worked between her and Shaun Murphy if everybody had just left them alone.

Delia took a deep breath and tried to banish the image of her handsome husband. Correction— former husband. Their marriage had lasted only a few hours, so why did she still picture herself as Shaun's seventeen-year-old, starry-eyed bride? It was ridiculous.

She'd been sure their love would last a lifetime, until her father had interfered. All he'd had to do was make a few threats and throw enough money at the problem for Shaun to walk away as if he'd never pledged his undying love.

"So, how's business?" Bianca asked pleasantly, jarring Delia back to the present.

"Good. We're already busy. Once school is out for the summer on the Mainland we'll get even busier. Every kid and his brother want to learn to surf."

"I still don't know how you teach anybody to balance on that cumbersome board the way you do," Juliet chimed in. "It looks really hard—and danger-ous."

"Not if you watch for rip currents and know what you're doing. Of course, I wouldn't try it on a rocky coast like this one, but it's wonderful under the right conditions. Catching the perfect wave and shooting the curl is a thrill like nothing else."

Bianca chuckled. "Oh, I don't know about that!"

Dark eyes twinkling, Portia and Rissa exchanged

knowing glances and quiet giggles. The twins were so in tune with each other they didn't need to say a word to communicate.

"Being madly in love with Leo doesn't count, Bianca." Juliet was grinning and rosy-cheeked. "Besides, my Brandon is much better looking than your Leo."

Bianca gave her baby sister a playful whack on the arm and shook her head. "He is not."

Delia wanted to join in the merriment but found it impossible to think of good-looking men without picturing Shaun, with his short, black hair, intense blue eyes and that five-o'clock shadow he never seemed able to shave off completely. And his smile. Oh, his smile. When he'd looked at her and flashed that killer smile she'd melted like a scoop of ice cream on a sizzling beach.

A sizzling beach was exactly where she belonged, and as soon as possible, she affirmed silently. When her father had shipped her off to the Islands to isolate her, he'd sent her to a place where she'd truly found her paradise on earth. Maybe God did work in mysterious ways, just as Aunt Winnie had always claimed.

And speaking of her aunt… Delia smiled as an older, distinguished-looking woman in a finely tailored, ivory silk suit approached. "There you all are!"

Delia briefly kissed her aunt's sweetly scented cheek and noticed how chilly her skin was. "You shouldn't have gone with us to the cemetery, Aunt Winnie. You're still freezing."

"Nonsense. You girls are dears but I wish you wouldn't treat me as if I were your grandfather's age. Unlike Howard, there are a lot of good years left in me." She smoothed the hair sleekly tucked into a chignon at her nape. "Even if there is a smidgen of gray in my hair."

"You're perfect," Delia said. "Someday I want you to come to Hawaii to visit me. The islands are really beautiful, even in the rainy season."

"Maine is beautiful, too," Winnie countered. "It's just a different kind of beauty. Like the roses in my garden. They may come in different colors and sizes but they're all gorgeous."

That reminded Delia of a famous line from *Romeo and Juliet.* "'That which we call a rose, by any other name would smell as sweet.'"

Winnie smiled, clearly delighted. "Exactly." She gestured toward the formal dining room. "Shall we? I have everything laid out on the table. I want each of you to have some keepsakes to remember Trudy by."

"I wish I could recall more about Mother than what you've told us over the years," Delia confessed. "It seems like such a waste to have found out she was alive, only to lose her again before we had a chance to even get acquainted."

Winnie sobered. "I know. But the Good Lord knows best. We can't always have everything we want in life."

Bianca came up behind them as they turned to move into the dining room. Speaking softly, she leaned close to Winnie's ear and said, "Sometimes, if we wait, the things we wish for do come to us. I understand you and Tate Connolly have been seen sharing romantic, candlelit dinners at the Coastal Inn."

When she saw a becoming blush brighten her aunt's features, Delia grinned. "Do tell? I can see I've been missing out on important family gossip." She glanced at the sister who had revealed Winnie's happy secret. "Why didn't you tell me, Bianca?"

"Because she was too caught up in dreaming of marrying Leo to think of anything else," Juliet offered. "I don't know how she manages to concentrate on her legal work back in Boston with all those stars in her eyes." The youngest sister struck a pose and mimicked, "I'm sorry, Your Honor, I'd have had that brief ready but I was so busy choosing my wedding gown and flowers it just slipped my mind."

"Oh, hush," Bianca said as Delia and the others laughed heartily. "I'm not the only one with stars in my eyes. I don't know why you're all teasing me. Portia, Rissa and Juliet are just as bad. This is not a contest to see who can make it to the altar first, you know."

Moments later, a stricken look came over Bianca, and Delia knew she had belatedly realized her faux pas. Rather than show her true feelings and spoil the lighthearted moment, Delia made a silly face. "In that case, I've already won. I beat you all by twelve years. Just don't start counting anniversaries or I'll lose my status, okay?"

That said, she stood tall, sidled past Aunt Winnie and led the way into the formal dining room. No way was she going to cry. Shedding tears for what might have been was as stupid as trying to surf on a beach where there was minimal wave action. Some goals were simply unrealistic. A Blanchard woman like her, looking for happiness with the likes of Shaun Murphy, was a perfect example of an impossible dream.

A dream she had long since abandoned.

Delia reacted from habit and took her usual place at the enormous mahogany dining table. Miranda, the eldest and shyest of the sisters was on her left. Bianca, the next oldest, sat on her right. Across from them, Delia's three younger sisters, Portia, Rissa and Juliet, sat next to Aunt Winnie. Their father, Ronald, Winnie's only sibling, had come as far as the arched doorway but had hung back there, obviously ill at ease and choosing not to join the group of women.

Delia eyed him surreptitiously. The others might have missed noticing the change in him because they saw him more often than she did, but she could easily tell how much he'd suffered since Trudy's funeral. Though he may not have shown any love for their late mother in life, he was definitely mourning for her now. How puzzling...

She glanced around the table as she absentmindedly smoothed the ecru lace cloth covering the lustrous, dark wood of the antique table. Except for

Juliet, who had been a baby at the time, they had all shed plenty of childhood tears over the loss of their mother. Twenty-some years ago they had been told that Trudy had died in a tragic auto accident. Finding out a few months ago that she was alive, then going through the trauma of losing her again, was surreal.

Delia was still struggling to believe that their mother had not only been living for all those intervening years, she'd spent most of them confined to a mental institution! No matter what Ronald's motives may have been at the time of their mother's initial illness, Delia couldn't excuse him for lying to his children about her. If, instead of postpartum depression, poor Trudy had suffered from something like cancer or heart disease, they would have been told the truth and could have comforted her, could have encouraged her to perhaps find healing.

Instead, Ronald had chosen to use Trudy's illness as an excuse to send her away from her family forever and thereby punish her for her marital indiscretions.

Sadly, Trudy hadn't been the only one to suffer. Her daughters had, too. Those years were lost to them all and now it was too late to do anything but divvy up the meager remnants of Trudy's sad life. If, as the Bible said, even a sparrow couldn't fall without God knowing and caring, why had He let her mother languish in a hospital like that when her children needed her? It just wasn't fair.

Delia was so immersed in retrospection that she jumped when the buzzer for the gate sounded. They

all did. Winnie started to rise, then paused when
Ronald said, "Stay there and finish what you're
doing. I'll see to it."

Curious, everyone listened for clues as to who
their caller might be. Blanchard manor was perched
on a cliff overlooking the ocean and was therefore
subject to being battered by terrible storms off the
North Atlantic. Delia and the others knew that only
the most intrepid New Englander would be out and
about on a foul day like this, even though the weather
wasn't quite as blustery and icy in May as it had been
a few months before.

In the background, Ronald's voice sounded
subdued as he spoke into the intercom, then released
the locked gate to admit their caller.

Soon, he was answering a knock on the front
door. The other male voice they overheard speaking
was almost stentorian, as if the person were enacting
a dramatic scene from *Hamlet* or *Richard III*.

Delia heard the man say, "Terrible shock, terrible
shock, my boy. We're so sorry. It must have been the
worst day of your life."

True to her reputation as the most daring of the six,
Delia rose from the table and started toward the door.

"Who is it?" Juliet called after her.

Delia peered around the corner into the entry hall,
then looked back at the others and shrugged. "I don't
have a clue. I don't think I've ever seen him before."

"Let me see." Juliet joined her. She was scowling
when she turned to Aunt Winnie and the others.
"Hmm. I don't know him, either."

"Then I guess we'll all have to have a look," Winnie said. Behind her, Portia and Rissa crowded closer to peek, too. Only Miranda held back.

Crowded by her sisters, Delia was forced to either step around the corner into view or be squashed against the door frame. She made the most graceful entrance she could manage, under the circumstances, and arrived with a stutter step just as the older man at the door was quoting, "'...such stuff as dreams are made on...,' eh?"

"The Tempest," Delia said, smiling and advancing to allow her sisters and her aunt enough room to join her. "Act four, scene one."

The distinguished, elderly gentleman's countenance immediately brightened. He looked past Ronald and smiled at Delia, his gray eyes misting behind his bifocals. "So, she knows her Shakespeare, just like her mother used to. Well done. And these lovely ladies must be her sisters."

"Yes," Ronald said, looking less than thrilled to be a party to their meeting.

"They mostly favor your coloring, with that dark hair and those big brown eyes, except—" the stranger cleared his throat as if he were fighting strong emotion "—that pretty blond one looks exactly like our Trudy did at that age."

The slim, silver-haired woman who stood beside him clutched his arm with a gloved hand, her lower lip quivering with emotion.

He laid his hand over hers and gave it a pat before he announced, "I'm your grandfather, Stanley. And this is your grandmother, Eleanor. Your mother, Gertrude—Trudy—was our daughter."

Suddenly, Delia wished she were still seated because her knees were definitely wobbling the way they did after catching a particularly harrowing wave. *Grandparents?* All this time she'd assumed that Howard Blanchard was their only living grand-parent and now... It was almost too much to fathom.

Ronald found his voice, cleared his throat and began to make proper introductions. "Girls, I'd like you to meet Mr. and Mrs. Hall, your mother's parents."

As Ronald had worked his way through all six of his daughters and Winnie, Eleanor had stepped forward to give each of them hugs. Delia had accepted the overture easily because of her years among the demonstrative Hawaiians but the others had remained rather stiff, especially Miranda.

Knowing her eldest sister's strong preference for solitude and private space, Delia had quickly inter-vened to spare Miranda from having to cope with too much overt affection, particularly from a stranger.

"Let Father take your coats." She passed Eleanor's wool wrap to Ronald, then grasped the older woman's thin arm and steered her toward the dining room as if she were the hostess rather than a fellow visitor.

"We were just going through some of our mother's things. Perhaps you'd like to join us," Delia said.

Eleanor agreed. "I do want to get to know you all better. Stanley and I would have dropped by sooner if we'd known." Her voice broke. "We were out of the country when…when Trudy passed away. We came as quickly as we could."

"How did you hear? Who contacted you?"

Eleanor sighed deeply. "No one. We read it in the newspaper. The story was apparently picked up by the wire services. If the Blanchard name wasn't newsworthy we might not have found out at all. We could hardly believe it was true when we read the details." Tears glistened in her green eyes.

Delia was instantly empathetic. "My sisters and I are having trouble making sense of everything, ourselves. It's like a bad dream. I keep thinking I'll wake up any minute and find out it's all a nightmare."

"I know," Eleanor said softly. "When Trudy called…"

Delia interrupted. "She what?"

"She telephoned us," Eleanor said. "We hadn't heard from her in years, and then, out of the blue, she called. She sounded wonderful. Perhaps a bit harried but otherwise quite well."

"Did you see her?"

"Unfortunately, no." The older woman sniffled, then held her chin high as if exemplary posture, alone, would sustain her. "We were hoping to. She said she was calling from our winter home in Santa Barbara."

"California? Why would she go way out there?" Delia asked before realizing that the call must have occurred around the time when Trudy had visited her former lover, Arthur Sinclair—Juliet's biological father—to ask him for financial assistance.

"I don't know," Eleanor answered. "She didn't say. By the time Stanley and I arrived there, Trudy was gone. When I think of how close we came to seeing her again, it breaks my heart."

Delia squeezed Eleanor's hand, hoping to console her in her time of grief.

"Both my poor girls were hopelessly lost to me," Eleanor continued. "That's another reason why I want so badly to get to know my granddaughters."

"*Both* your girls? Mother wasn't an only child?" Delia was flabbergasted.

"No. We have—we *had* two daughters. Your mother was the elder."

Delia stared at Ronald with condemnation. "I don't understand why Father never told us anything about your side of the family."

"Don't be too hard on him," Eleanor said. "Stanley and I owe him a lot. When he was a young man he used his trust fund to save our literary press, you know, in spite of his father's vehement disapproval of the whole affair."

"No, I didn't know, but I can see we have a lot to talk about."

"That we do," Stanley said, hanging back with Ronald. "We were devastated when Trudy dropped out of school to marry your father here, but you girls are the treasure that resulted. He must be very proud."

Proud of most of us, Delia thought. She was the

black sheep of the family and always had been. Perhaps she also had more in common with her mother than she'd imagined.

She guided Eleanor to the massive dining room table and seated her before taking her own chair once again. "There isn't much left of mother's jewelry or mementos but if there's anything here that means a lot to you, my sisters and I want you to have it." She refrained from adding that very little was special to them because of their long estrangement. Bianca had saved a few things and Juliet had unearthed some others in the attic, but most of the items arrayed on the table had come from Aunt Winnie.

Eleanor laid her clutch on the table, removed her dove-gray kid gloves and placed them beside the bag. Her delicate fingers traced the outline of a gold chain that lay in front of her and she pushed aside a few small photographs. Then, she folded her hands in her lap and sighed. "I'm afraid I don't see the locket." Her eyes misted as she glanced back at her husband. "It's not here, Stanley."

He nodded slowly. "That is a shame."

"What locket?" Delia asked.

Eleanor sniffled demurely. "It was heart-shaped. My mother gave it to me on my sixteenth birthday and I passed it on to Trudy. She never took it off, at least not while she was young. She promised me she'd treasure it always."

A sharp intake of breath caused everyone to stare at Miranda. "That's right! I remember how Mother always wore that locket. I used to love to read the inscription on the back when I was little."

"'To thine own self be true,'" Eleanor quoted. "From *Hamlet*."

"Then it must be here," Delia said, sifting through the small pile of belongings. "We added everything we got back from the coroner's office, too, didn't we?"

"Except for the ruined silk scarf," Winnie said pensively. "I certainly don't recall seeing the locket, although I do remember Trudy wearing it long ago."

Delia got to her feet. "I'll call the coroner's office. Maybe it's still there. It certainly can't hurt to ask."

"I hate to have you go to all that trouble but I really would like to have it back—or at least know that one of you girls would treasure it as much as your mother once did," Eleanor said.

Delia excused herself, went into the den to make the call in private and returned quickly.

All eyes were on her as she reentered the dining room. She shrugged sadly. "They say there was no jewelry on our mother when she was picked up." She looked to her newfound grandmother. "I'm sorry, Eleanor. I guess your locket is lost."

The older woman blinked and stared, obviously engrossed in thought. The seconds ticked by slowly. Finally, she said, "Trudy would never have parted with that locket. It was a solemn pact between us. She wouldn't have broken that trust. Not for anything."

"She was sick a long time," Delia argued, trying to be sensible and gentle at the same time. "Maybe

she changed. Anyone would have under such stress-
ful circumstances."

Eleanor was adamant. "Trudy swore to me that
she'd wear my locket to the grave. If she wasn't
buried wearing it, maybe she wasn't buried at all."

In the background, Ronald inhaled sharply and
sagged against the wall. Stanley half supported him
as he frowned at his wife. "Are you thinking what
I'm thinking?"

Nodding, Eleanor looked around the table at the
sisters until her gaze came to rest on Juliet. "Trudy
resembled you, as we said, but so did her sister,
Genie. My girls were often mistaken for twins, even
though they were born at different times. The simi-
larity was only skin deep, however. Genie's personality was twisted. I hate to admit it but she wasn't a
very moral person. She gambled, used illegal drugs
and who knows what else. And she was mercenary
to the nth degree."

Eleanor turned to Ronald. "Is it possible that the
woman who was identified as Trudy was actually
Genie? It would explain why she didn't have the
locket."

"Wait a minute." Delia was dumbfounded. The
way Eleanor had been referring to her younger
daughter, she'd assumed the woman had passed away
long ago. Now, she realized otherwise. She looked
from Eleanor to Ronald and began to frown. "What
would this Genie person be doing in your house,
Father? You never mentioned even knowing her."

She paused and studied his pained expression.

He didn't speak. When he looked away and refused to continue to make eye contact, Delia was taken aback. "You *did* know her, didn't you?"

Mind racing, she remembered a lock of pale hair bound in a faded pink ribbon. Trudy's hair. It was lying on the table amid the other mementos. The answer to their riddle could be right there before them, thanks to recent developments in scientific testing methods.

Delia's trembling fingers reached for the lock of hair. She cradled it gently in her palm, displaying it for everyone to see. "All right. We can settle this once and for all with a DNA test on Mother's hair. I don't care what it costs or how long it takes. I'm going to find out precisely who we buried last month."

Winnie's voice was uneven. "And if it wasn't Trudy?"

"If it wasn't, then I'm going to dig until I learn what an imposter was doing in this house and what she was after."

"You'd better leave this to the authorities," Winnie said firmly. "I don't want you getting hurt."

Delia shook her head emphatically. "No way. I've lost my mother twice, already. If there's even a slight chance she's still alive, I'm going to be personally involved in the investigation. First thing tomorrow I'll drive into town and get the process started."

"And then what?" Winnie asked.

"Then, I'll do what I do when I'm waiting for the

perfect wave. I'll mark time and paddle till it's time to stand up and go with the flow."

"Even if there's a chance it will be dangerous?" Juliet asked breathlessly.

Delia knew exactly what Winnie and her baby sister were worried about. There had been far too many near-fatal accidents involving their immediate family in the past few months for it to have been co-incidental. Still, she wasn't going to let herself be deterred. "Yes. Absolutely. I'm not afraid."

From the doorway, Stanley's voice boomed. "Brava! Trudy named you well. Cordelia means 'the wise one,' you know."

Delia stood tall and squared her shoulders. "Yes, I know. I also know what eventually happened to poor Cordelia in Shakespeare's play, but nothing terrible is going to happen to me. Unlike the jealous, wicked daughters of King Lear, my sisters are smart, loving women. And they're on my side, every one of them."

Letting her gaze travel around the table and rest for a moment on each of her siblings, Delia knew she spoke the absolute truth. The Blanchard sisters might not all display the same audacity she did but they were unified by their mutual love. If she needed support they would back her up. Period. Theirs was an alliance formed over the course of troubled childhood years and strengthened by their need to rely upon one another.

In a perverse way, the negative actions and lies of their embittered, workaholic father had forged bonds between his daughters that were as strong as steel.

Delia's heart swelled with love as she considered her siblings. Never before had she been so proud to be one of the Blanchard sisters.

TWO

Shaun Murphy's strong, calloused hands tightened on the steering wheel of the Murphy Woodworkers' company pickup. Although he hadn't been back in Stoneley for very long, he was ready to hit the road again at the first opportunity.

He wouldn't have returned at all if his ailing father hadn't desperately needed his help in the woodworking shop. Business had fallen off to the point where the shop was barely solvent and Shaun couldn't bring himself to turn down his dad's plea for assistance, even though it meant he'd have to coexist with the one family he despised.

To be more precise, it was Ronald Blanchard he hated. The others he could take or leave—preferably leave—with the exception of Delia. The last he'd heard, she was all the way over in Hawaii so at least he'd be spared the risk of accidentally running into her.

His hands fisted on the wheel. He'd nearly choked when Miranda Blanchard had phoned and offered him a repair job at the estate. If there had been any way to turn her down without jeopardizing his father's future livelihood he would have. In a heartbeat. But small, struggling businesses like Murphy Woodworkers didn't buck the Blanchards. When one of them wanted something done, you didn't question it—you simply obeyed. It was their textile mill that kept the local economy ticking like a fine watch and everybody knew it.

Shaun stopped at the locked gate fronting the Blanchard estate and rolled down the truck's window. Miranda hadn't given him the admittance code but she had told him she could release the lock from the house when he announced his arrival. He leaned out and pressed the intercom button.

"It's Murphy Woodworkers," he said loudly. "Ms. Blanchard is expecting me."

The lock clicked and the gate slowly swung open. Shaun rolled his window back up while he made a careful turn onto the serpentine drive leading to the huge stone mansion. The worst of the latest storm had passed in the night but the ground was still wet and a coastal fog bank made it hard to see clearly, even in the morning light. That was Maine for you. Then again, if a person wanted sun and dry warmth all the time they belonged in Southern Arizona, which was probably where he'd be right now if he hadn't had to come home to help his dad.

Rather than chance running off the paved roadway in the fog and damaging the elaborate gardens surrounding the mansion, Shaun kept to the center of the drive. Shafts of sunlight broke through here and there, making him squint.

Suddenly, beams of blinding brightness arced across his path. He hit the brakes and started to skid.

Just ahead, the beams swung to one side and Shaun caught a glimpse of the side of a red compact car as it careened off the road and plowed headlong into a substantial grouping of rhododendron bushes!

To his relief, there was no tree trunk amid the vegetation to cause the driver harm. That feeling of gratitude was short-lived, however. This was Blanchard property. It didn't matter who had run off the road or whose fault it was, he was liable to be blamed.

He shut off the truck's engine, climbed out and jogged to where the car had come to rest. It wasn't one of those expensive luxury models the Blanchards usually drove so maybe he'd be lucky enough to escape with a handshake and a few pleasantries.

"Hey, I'm really sorry!" he called. "Are you okay?" All Shaun could see was the left side of a beige, hooded jacket and a shoulder bumping repeatedly against the door.

"Door's stuck." The driver's voice was muted by the closed vehicle.

"Hang on. I'll have you out of there in a jiffy." He gave the handle a jerk and it worked. "There you go."

Holding the door he stepped back. The driver swiveled in the seat, extended her shapely legs and looked up at him.

He gaped. There, in all her glory, was the woman

who had heartlessly abandoned him on their wedding night twelve years ago, without so much as a word—or even a goodbye note.

Delia's eyes widened. By the time she'd looked Shaun over from head to toe, it was an effort to muster enough breath to inquire, "What are you doing here?"

"I could ask you the same thing," Shaun replied tersely.

She quickly regained her poise in the face of his challenging tone. "This is my family's estate. I *belong* here, remember?"

"And I don't, is that your point? Well, it so happens your sister called and hired me to fix the library doors."

"Which sister?"

"Miranda. Why?"

"No reason." Delia would have suspected matchmaking if Aunt Winnie or Juliet had been involved. Miranda, however, was anything but meddlesome, so meeting Shaun like this must have truly been an accident. In more ways than one.

Trying to ignore his ruggedly imposing presence, Delia got to her feet, pushed past him and stood back to examine her car. "It looks like it's okay. I suppose I should be thankful."

"Thankful you didn't get somebody killed, you mean? What were you doing driving so fast in the fog? You're familiar with the weather up here. You should know better."

She arched a dark eyebrow. "So are you. I wasn't the one hogging the middle of the road."

"Yeah, well, I was in a hurry to get to the house and get to work."

She glanced at the truck. It had obviously seen better days. "Since when do you work for your father?"

"Since his arthritis flared up. Some days it's so bad he can hardly move."

That took some of the ire out of her. "I'm sorry. I didn't know."

"We're coping. What about you? How come you're slumming in Stoneley? I thought you lived in Samoa or some exotic place like that."

"Hawaii," Delia said, positive he was just trying to annoy her. Everybody in Stoneley knew she'd been shipped off to Hawaii for college and had stayed there after graduation. Leave it to Shaun to pretend he didn't know or care where she'd gone.

"Okay, Hawaii," he grumbled, eyeing the car. "I know you didn't drive here in *that*."

"You always were a smart man," she countered.

He huffed with evident disgust. "That's debatable."

"Maybe I should have said you had a smart mouth."

"Takes one to know one."

"Touché." Delia had to work to suppress a smile in spite of his clear animosity. She and Shaun had always enjoyed taunting each other and their rapid repartee brought back fond memories.

He struck a nonchalant pose, his hands stuffed into the pockets of his denim jacket. "So, where were you headed when you decided to take a detour into the shrubbery?"

"To town." She glanced at the small envelope lying on the front seat of her car. It contained the precious lock of Trudy's hair. "I'm sort of on a mission."

"Sounds important. Of course, everything the Blanchards do is important, right?"

"There's no need to be sarcastic," she said. "Guess I'd better get going."

"You sure that car's okay?"

"Probably, if you don't count the scratches. They're really going to sock it to me when I turn it in at the airport." She thought she saw him flinch.

"How much longer are you staying?"

"Maybe a week. Maybe less. As soon as my business for the family is finished I'll be heading home."

"Good."

Delia tensed. "Good?"

"I didn't think you liked it here."

"You've got that right." She eyed the drive she'd recently traversed. "So, are you going to just stand there giving me trouble or are you going to get back in your truck and scram before my father comes by on his way to work and starts asking us what happened?"

"You aren't going to tell him?"

Delia shook her head. "Why should I? If anybody

notices that the bushes look funny I'll just say I accidentally ran off the drive, which is the truth."

"Thanks."

"Hey, I'm not doing it for you, I'm doing it for your poor father. I figure he has enough troubles already without my adding to them."

For a moment she thought she saw a flash of relief cross Shaun's handsome face. Then he stood at attention and gave her a mocking salute. "It's been a pleasure running into you, Ms. Blanchard. Or should I say *almost* running into you?"

With that he wheeled around and jogged back to his truck.

Delia bit her lower lip to keep from calling after him to get the last word. The less she and Shaun Murphy had to do with each other, the better off they'd both be.

She didn't know how deeply their chance meeting had affected him but it had shaken her all the way to her core. Watching him depart had tied her stomach in a knot and left her mouth dry. She was going to have to get a grip on herself or people were going to start imagining she still cared for him.

She didn't, of course. It was ridiculous to think that a sensible, independent woman like her could be influenced by a boyish smile and a square jaw perpetually covered with the light shadow of a beard. Her world might not be filled with playboys in Armani suits anymore but she wasn't going to let herself be swayed by flannel and denim, either. Not even when that flannel covered a set of muscles to die for.

Fond memories were all right if kept in their proper place, in their proper perspective, Delia reasoned. Shaun Murphy had vowed he loved her and then not only hadn't come after her when she'd been dragged home from their interrupted honeymoon, he'd never even tried to contact her again. As far as she was concerned, the man was history.

She just wished her history wasn't still so appealing.

Knowing that DNA identification usually took several weeks, Delia was amazed when a clerk from the police department lab called on Friday to tell her that the test results had been faxed in. Apparently, Blanchard money was the perfect oil for the rusty wheels of bureaucracy.

She thought about notifying her father and letting him pick up the official report on his way home from work, then decided against it and headed into town. Ronald hadn't acted as if he'd wanted her to go ahead with the DNA test in the first place so she was determined to handle all the details herself. She couldn't decide whether her father was simply afraid of what he might learn or if he subconsciously *wanted* Trudy to be the deceased. It was hard to imagine why he would, but then she didn't have a clue what made the man tick. She had never understood him.

Driving through Stoneley made her a bit melancholy. The town, which had been founded in the mid-1600s, was a peaceful place with a year-round population hovering around ten thousand, give or take the tourists and others who were just passing through. The churches were the cornerstones of the community, especially Unity Christian where her family attended, and there wasn't much big-city-like conflict. At least there hadn't been until the recent traumas involving the Blanchards.

She cruised slowly down the picturesque main street past antique shops, the bookstore and the retro five-and-dime which bragged that everything was just as it had been at the turn of the century.

It looked as if the theater was trying to capitalize on the nostalgia craze, too, because the marquee boasted that it was showing a series of black-and-white romantic comedies from the 1940s.

She recalled the summer when she had snuck away every chance she got to secretly meet Shaun in that very theater. Their elopement plans had been formulated in the last row of red velour seats, right below the projection booth. She could almost smell the popcorn.

"We can't get married until you're finished with high school," Shaun had insisted. "Your education is important."

Delia remembered leaning against the armrest that had separated them and clinging to him as his strong left arm had encircled her shoulders. "But, we love each other. That's all that matters."

"No, it isn't. Your family is going to pitch a royal fit, anyway. We don't want to give them any more to yell about than we have to."

Even at seventeen, Delia had known that Shaun was right. After all, he was two years older than she was and already a man of the world. He had a job, a future. One she fully intended to share with him.

"All right," she'd conceded. "I can't very well run off and get married without the groom, can I?"

That silly comment had made him chuckle. He'd pulled her closer and stolen a kiss—one of many.

"Knowing you, Delia, anything is possible." He'd sobered. "You're not afraid? Of your father, I mean?"

"No. There's nothing he can do to me that will ever make me stop loving you," she had vowed.

What a fool. Unshed tears blurred Delia's vision as she drove on past the theater. Realizing she was a road hazard when she was so upset, she pulled into the first available parking spot.

"Stupid, stupid, stupid," she muttered, hitting the steering wheel with her palms. Reliving the past accomplished nothing. All it did was make her cry and leave her with a sinus headache.

She huffed in self-derision. If she wasn't battling a literal headache she was fighting a figurative one. The sooner she picked up those test results and got things settled, the sooner she could escape Stoneley and the bittersweet memories of her youth.

Accidentally running into Shaun at the estate the other morning must have triggered all these emotions, she concluded. She was over him and had been for a long, long time. That's all there was to it.

Oh yeah? Then why was she crying?

If I knew the answer to that, Delia thought, *I'd be halfway back to feeling normal, assuming I'd recognize normalcy if I saw it. After all, I'm a Blanchard.*

Rather than have someone who knew her question her red eyes and upset demeanor, she donned dark glasses, picked up her purse and hurried down the cracked sidewalk toward the police department. The sooner she got this over with, the better off she'd be.

Shaun had just finished having breakfast at the Clambake Café and was heading for his truck when he noticed a red compact car cruising through the intersection of Blueberry and Main Streets. He didn't know why that particular car had caught his eye but it had. Since when did he care about stupid little cars with scratches on the sides? he mused.

"Since I saw Delia driving one," he answered drily.

He jogged to the street corner in time to see the red car swing into an empty spot up the block. The driver climbed out. His pulse accelerated. It *was* Delia.

Hmm. It looked as if she was headed for the police department. Shaun squinted and shaded his eyes. *The question was— What for?*

He crossed the street and continued to watch the double, glass-topped doors until Delia emerged several minutes later. He hadn't intended to let her know he was nearby but when he saw her stop and lean against the redbrick wall fronting the office as if she were unsteady on her feet, he immediately started toward her.

There was a single sheet of white paper in her hand. It was shaking like a leaf in a nor'easter.

She didn't look up when he joined her so he paused and announced his presence. "Delia?"

Her face tilted up slowly. Shaun didn't have to see her eyes behind the dark glasses to know she was distraught—he could feel it in his bones. "What is it? What's wrong?"

"DNA," she said.

"Whose?" He saw her swallow hard and forced himself to wait for her answer when what he wanted to do was grasp her shoulders and shake it out of her. Her lips were trembling. So was the rest of her. Whatever had her this upset had to be catastrophic.

"I don't know whose," she finally said, passing him the sheet of paper. "Read it for yourself."

Shaun scanned the report but didn't notice anything unusual about it. "Trudy Blanchard?"

"Yes. My mother. I'm sure you heard. We held her funeral about a month ago. It was quite an elegant affair."

"No, I hadn't heard about it. I'm sorry." He chanced touching her elbow as a gesture of genuine concern and was surprised she didn't rebuff him. "I haven't been back in Stoneley very long and, well, nobody talks about your family to me."

"That's certainly understandable," she said. "I think I need to sit down."

Shaun guided her to a nearby decorative iron bench. "Want to tell me what's got you so upset?"

"Yes. No." She made a wry face. "I guess it would be nice to have somebody to talk through it with before I go back to the house."

He perched beside her, taking care not to get too close. "Go ahead."

"She wasn't my mother," Delia whispered, staring at the report. "The woman we buried wasn't my mother."

"Then who was she?"

Delia shook her head. "I don't know for sure. I think she may have been my aunt, Genie."

"I didn't know you had an aunt Genie."

"Neither did I until a few days ago."

"That's crazy."

"Yeah, tell me about it. I didn't know my mother's parents were alive, either, and now I have three times the grandparents I thought I had." She sighed. "The Halls, Stanley and Eleanor, seem like really nice people. It's a relief to know someone besides Grandfather Howard."

Shaun huffed. "I can sure understand *that*."

"Well said. There are times when I wonder how I ended up with so many odd relatives—except my sisters and Aunt Winnie, of course. They're dears."

Glancing at the report again, Shaun looked puzzled. "It says here that even though the DNA doesn't match, it was close. Is that why you think the person was a relative?"

Delia nodded and sighed deeply. "Yes. My new

grandparents told us that Aunt Genie and my mother looked very much alike so I suppose a mistaken ID is possible. Genie had to be the body in the library. It couldn't have been anyone else."

"Sounds like the plot of an old mystery novel," he remarked. "You know, the part about the body in the library?" He paused and began to frown. "Hey, wait a minute. Is that when you got that bullet hole in the door that I was hired to fix? I just assumed it had been damaged because of someone's carelessness with firearms. I never dreamed there was a real murder there. Who did it?"

"Actually, the police are still trying to figure that out," Delia said. "I think they're leaning toward Grandfather Howard, although I can't imagine he'd be clever enough to shoot and then remember to dispose of the weapon. Not in his present state of confusion."

"Alzheimer's. I had heard about that," Shaun said. "So, what are you going to do now?"

"Go home and break the news to everybody, I guess," Delia said. "It's going to be quite a shock."

"Especially to your maternal grandparents. Are they staying at the estate, too?"

"No. Aunt Winnie offered to accommodate them but they said they didn't want to be in the same house with Howard. I don't blame them. He was terribly cruel to my mother in the past and his disease has removed his inhibitions. Half the time, he thinks poor Juliet is Mother and pitches terrible fits when he sees her. It's scary."

"Are you sure you're safe there?" Shaun was sorry the minute the words were out of his mouth because they revealed far too much personal concern. "Any of you, I mean," he quickly added.

"We're fine. After the shooting, Father changed the combination that activates the alarm system, just in case. And Grandfather's nurse, Peg Henderson, is with him almost constantly. She sedates him, for his own good, if he gets too wild. She's really patient with him. I sure wouldn't want her job."

"Neither would I." Shaun relaxed, one arm passing behind Delia along the back of the iron bench without touching her. "You look like you're feeling better."

"I am. Thanks."

"Do you want me to drive you home?"

"No. I have my car. I just needed to calm down." She stood. "I'd better be going. Aunt Winnie will wonder what's taking me so long. I don't want her to worry."

Shaun rose, too, stuffing his hands into the pockets of his jeans. "Well, take care."

"I will. No more driving into the bushes, I promise. Will you be coming to work on the door soon?"

"I ordered a special, high-grade mahogany veneer for patching," he said. "It hasn't arrived yet."

"Oh. Well, if I don't see you again…" She held out her hand.

Shaun didn't want to touch her but he saw no polite way of refusing so he grasped her extended hand, fully intending to give it a quick shake and then release it. Instead, when he felt her icy fingers, he covered their clasped hands with his other. "You're freezing. Are you sure you're all right?"

"Thin blood from living in the tropics," Delia explained. "I'll be fine as soon as I can get out of Maine."

"You're leaving soon, right?" He'd been dragging his feet on the repair job rather than work in the house while she was present. The last thing he wanted was to be constantly reminded of their painful past.

"Yes," Delia said, slipping her hand from his. "I was only staying until we got these results back. I really never dreamed the test would turn out this way." She smiled slightly and stepped back. "Goodbye, Shaun."

He increased the distance. "Bye, Delia." There was nothing more to say. Nothing he dared even think. Considering the way his teeth were set and his muscles were twitching, the less said, the better.

There was no longer any doubt in Shaun's mind that he'd been wise to avoid Delia. He didn't care that the special order mahogany for the door had come in days ago—he was not going near the Blanchard estate again until she was gone.

THREE

To Delia's consternation, everyone in her family had been too stunned by the news about the DNA to think clearly, let alone act on it quickly enough to suit her. That was why she had decided to delay her departure and take matters into her own hands. She'd found several probable addresses for Genie Hall on the Internet, had pocketed the only key that had been returned to the Blanchards by the coroner and had headed for the nearest, in upstate New York.

According to Eleanor, Genie had had no husband or children so Delia figured there would be no close survivors to object if she did a little harmless snooping. And maybe picked up some of Genie's DNA from her hairbrush, too, if possible, just to double-check identities.

Delia fingered the lone door key in her jacket pocket for the hundredth time. She'd hated deceiving her family by leading them to believe she was headed for Bangor to catch a plane for Hawaii, but the innocent ruse had been necessary. Even if her sisters had understood her motives, she knew her father would have tried to stop her from investigating. Keeping his family under his thumb was Ronald Blanchard's standard method of operation. After all, look what had happened to her poor, ill mother.

Cruising slowly along the tree-lined street in the upscale neighborhood west of Lake Champlain, Delia found the address she was looking for and parked in front of the ultramodern building complex. If this was where Genie had actually lived, her aunt had done well for herself in spite of Eleanor's claim that the woman was perpetually in trouble.

In view of that, Delia suspected she might have chosen the wrong address. Well, she'd soon know. If this wasn't Genie's home, the door key wouldn't work and she'd simply proceed to the next place on her list.

Climbing out of the car, Delia straightened her cropped jacket over the designer jeans Juliet had insisted on giving her. She grabbed her shoulder bag from the front seat, took a deep breath and tossed her head to fluff her hair. Then she turned, crossed the sidewalk and started boldly up the front walk.

The burly, tattooed man who had been keeping watch on the condominium complex was so bored he was almost asleep. He caught a glimpse of movement, blinked and rubbed his eyes. *Finally. Some action.*

He got to his feet and stretched. Genie's other apartment, the one near the mental hospital in

Chicago, had clearly been abandoned so he'd concentrated his efforts at her New York State address. In the past month and a half he'd memorized the faces of all the residents. The dark-haired, younger woman entering the condo was definitely not Genie Hall but she was not one of the locals, either. Therefore, she would bear watching.

He clenched his fists. He'd let her get far enough ahead that she wouldn't notice him, then follow. A lot of money was riding on his success. He'd promised himself another week before giving up and writing off the debt and it looked as if his luck was about to change.

To Delia's relief the key opened the door. That meant she was on the right track but she was still going to try to get a hair sample or something. Having Genie's DNA would remove all doubt about the murder victim's identification.

Thankfully, there was no yellow plastic police department tape sealing off the apartment. She knew when and if there was an official search of her aunt's residence, some of the clues she was after would probably become evidence. There was no telling what kind of jumble the remaining items would be left in, either.

Hands resting on her shoulder bag, she spoke to the empty room. "Okay, Aunt Genie, what secrets were you hiding, huh? You might as well tell me because I'm going to turn this place upside down until I figure out what you've been up to."

Delia shivered slightly. She was talking to thin air. Maybe her mother wasn't the only family member who needed psychiatric care. She shoved the self-deprecating thought aside. Several of her sisters had confessed to having had similar notions recently and they were reasonably well-balanced women, although Rissa was being treated for depression and Miranda bordered on agoraphobia. It was actually pretty amazing how artistic and creative both women were despite their illnesses.

Considering her sisters led Delia's thoughts directly to their Aunt Winnie and made her smile.

"If Winnie were here she'd tell me to pray," Delia murmured, wishing she felt worthy of asking for God's guidance. As a six-year-old, she'd spent many tearful nights praying for her mother's return, to no avail, and the lack of an answer had undermined her faith. It had been a long time since she'd asked God for anything specific, let alone listened for His answer.

But He did answer me, didn't He? She was amazed that she hadn't realized that sooner. She slowly shook her head. Finding out that her mother was alive after all these years certainly wasn't the answer she'd expected but it was definitely an answer! Talk about a long delay.

Wandering into the bedroom, Delia scanned the expensive furnishings, assessed her options, then laid her purse on the satin comforter on the bed and began to look through the modern chest of drawers.

She found nothing but designer clothing and silky

nightgowns until she progressed to the dressing table and slid open a small drawer on the left side.

It was a treasure trove! Her trembling hands lifted a stack of faded, dog-eared photographs. She made room to spread them on the glass-topped vanity by shoving cosmetics and toiletries out of the way, then seated herself on the velvet-covered stool, facing the mirror.

Her breath immediately caught. "Trudy" was written on the back of the top photo, as clearly as if it had just been penned.

She turned the small photo over. Her heart pounded. It was the picture of a woman who looked enough like her sister Juliet to be her twin, except that the image had been disfigured.

Delia stared in disbelief. The woman's eyes had been poked out, apparently with a pencil point! Horrified, Delia could only whisper, "That's *sick*."

Looking away rather than make herself study the photo one second longer, she raised her eyes to the vanity mirror and felt her stomach lurch.

Standing directly behind her, blocking her escape, was an enormous man with a menacing expression and forearms tattooed so heavily it was hard to make out any bare skin. There was a black bandanna tied around his head. That, and the scar slashing his bristly cheek made him resemble a modern-day pirate.

Fright provided all the incentive she needed to whisper, "God help me!" and mean every word.

The man laughed coarsely. "Well, well. What have we here? You robbin' the place, lady?"

"No! I'm not a burglar," Delia insisted, whirling to face him. "Who are you?"

"None of your business. What're you doing here?"

"Why should I answer that?"

"Because I'll call building security if you don't."

Delia wished he would. "Fine. Do it. I have every right to be here. This is my aunt's condo."

"Oh yeah? Then you should know where she's hanging out these days."

"Genie is dead," Delia replied bluntly. "Was she a friend of yours?"

He seemed to take his time deciding what to do next. Finally, he nodded. "Yeah, she was. Okay. Suppose I buy your story. You say you're family so you'll do. You can pay me the money she owes me."

"I beg your pardon?"

The man laughed again, sounding even more sinister this time. "I see you ain't as bright as ole Genie was. I'll make it real simple. She owed me a bundle. I aim to collect. You look like you can afford to pay her debts."

The amount he then cited was enough to raise Delia's eyebrows. "I don't carry that kind of money on me." She eyed her purse on the bed and took a chance by offering, "Go ahead. Look for yourself if you don't believe me."

He shook his head. "Never mind. I'll give you twenty-four hours. Get it."

She decided it was wiser to stall than to try to slip past him and make a dash for her car. Judging by his obvious strength she wouldn't be able to break away if he laid a hand on her.

"Okay. Right here, same time tomorrow. How's that?" she said, hoping she didn't sound as frightened as she felt.

"Why not go to the bank right now and get started?"

"It's too late in the day," Delia said. "You know I can't get that much from an ATM, even if I go to more than one." Not to mention the fact that she didn't have nearly enough cash in her accounts, including savings.

"Okay," the thug said. "Tomorrow. But don't try nothing funny, you hear."

"I won't. You be here and you'll get your money." She straightened her spine to strengthen her courage. "Now, I suggest you get out of here before somebody spots you and really does call security. You don't exactly blend in, you know."

That made him chuckle. "Now you sound just like Genie used to. I'm kind of sorry she's gone. What'd she do, drive too fast and wreck her car or something?"

"No," Delia said boldly. "She was shot to death in the library of my father's house." To her surprise, the man blanched and started to back away.

"Okay. Tomorrow. You remember."

"I'm not likely to forget," Delia said, barely able to control her shaking.

As soon as he'd left the apartment she sank heavily onto the edge of the bed. This was the last place she wanted to be but she knew she had to force

herself to tarry long enough to make sure her antago-
nist was gone.

And then? Then, she'd gather up the horrible
photos and whatever else was in that drawer and
head for Stoneley as quickly as possible. She didn't
care if she had to drive all night.

For the first time in longer than she could
remember she was actually looking forward to being
inside the fortresslike walls of Blanchard manor.

The man hadn't looked in her purse so he didn't
know her name. That was one thing in her favor. All
she had to do to facilitate her escape was to be sure
no one followed her home.

Delia had managed to stay on the move for most
of the night. The few times that sleep had threatened
she'd taken short breaks for food and lots of coffee,
making sure that the places she stopped were well
lit and very public.

Constantly monitoring her rearview mirror had
shown no unusual traffic behind her and no cars had
stayed close enough to raise her suspicions.

It was just after dawn when she pulled up to the
iron gates of Blanchard manor, keyed in her code to
unlock them, and drove through as they swung open.
She sighed, feeling exhausted. Not only was she
unused to driving so much, she'd wasted a lot of
energy being nervous.

Rather than go to the extra trouble of driving
around back and putting her rental car in the garage
with the other Blanchard vehicles, she parked

directly in front of the house. It was so early that everybody was probably still in bed, Delia reasoned. That didn't matter one bit. She needed a shower and a long nap a lot worse than she needed her usual welcoming committee.

Not bothering to pull her suitcases out of the car's trunk, she grabbed her purse and started for the front door, absentmindedly counting the stone steps the way she always had as a child. Three, four, five...

The noise of an approaching engine caused her to pause and look back. She shaded her eyes against the rising sun and peered down the driveway. The sound reminded her of one of those really heavy motorcycles that thumped and roared instead of buzzing like a hornet.

Who did they know who rode a bike, let alone one like that? And how had anyone gotten into the secured estate? Could the rider have slipped through the gates behind her? Had she been so distracted that she'd driven off without waiting for them to close properly? Apparently so.

In a split second she knew who the intruder was! A black motorcycle roared into view, its rider leaning into a curve. He was as huge and imposing as his two-wheeled transportation.

Delia didn't have to see the tattoos on his forearms under his leather jacket to know that the burly man from Genie's condo had followed her! And she'd apparently been lax enough to let him sneak onto the grounds.

She spun, made a mad dash for the door, gripped the knob and twisted. It didn't give. Locked! Of course it was. No members of the household would be up this early. And except for the rental car's ignition key, which she still held in her hand, her keys were lost somewhere in the nether reaches of her copious shoulder bag.

She began to frantically paw through the contents of her purse. "Key! Where's my key?"

If she could just open the door she knew her presence would set off the burglar alarm and rouse everyone. Father had changed the alarm code after the intrusion and shooting in the library. She had no idea what new combinations of numbers he'd programmed into the alarm so, once the ringing began, she couldn't shut it off if she wanted to.

The keys remained elusive. The motorcycle was almost to the porch. *Now* what? Delia's head snapped around. The back door! Maybe Andre, the cook, had unlocked the kitchen. If she could slip in that way she could hit the panic button and it would have the same effect. Plus, if she remembered correctly, the house alarm would trigger an automatic response by the local police.

Feet flying, fatigue forgotten, Delia raced back down the steps at an angle, heading for the west corner of the house. Behind her, she heard the motorcycle rumble closer, then suddenly stop. Her senses were at their peak. Her pursuer was now on foot. And the rapid clomp of his boots told her he was closing in!

She shrieked when he grabbed her arm, twisting in his grip to partially face him. "Let me go!"

"Not on your life, lady. You think I'm stupid or something?"

Delia refused to tell him what she did think but her thoughts were far from ladylike, let alone civilized. Her upbringing had definitely not prepared her to face a crisis like this.

"Never mind what I think," she warned. "Let go of me or I'll scream my head off."

"Go ahead. Scream all you want," the man said with a leer that made the scar on his cheek form a slight arc. "Maybe somebody'll come to your rescue and *they'll* pay me. I don't care where the money comes from as long as I get it." He glanced at the mansion with clear disdain. "From the looks of this place, my fee would be pocket change."

Delia's heart sank. Her supposedly innocent deception had come home to bite her, hadn't it? Her family thought she'd gone to Hawaii, not upstate New York. What was her father going to say if he learned where she'd encountered this awful man?

She tried to speak normally. "Look, Mr. Whatever-your-name-is, I said I'd get you your money. I never said I wouldn't have to go somewhere else to lay my hands on it."

"Yeah, yeah. Don't you know it's not nice to lie?"

What could she say? Behind the man, Delia glimpsed a flash of light. The rising sun glinted off glass. A windshield. Help was coming! She didn't care who or what was approaching. She only knew that she'd soon have a witness and her attacker would be less likely to chance harming her any more than he already had.

Her obvious interest in the area directly behind him gave the man reason to turn, dragging her with him by the wrist. Delia cringed from the pain, trying to lag back.

She saw a familiar figure running toward them. *Shaun*. It was Shaun!

Her first reaction was relief. Concern for his safety quickly followed. Shaun was obviously in good physical shape but her attacker outweighed him by a ton. Poor Shaun was liable to get hurt— and it would be her fault.

All she had time for was a squeaky, "No! Don't!" before Shaun reached them.

His hands came together in front of him, connected with her attacker's grip in a scissorlike, upward motion and she was suddenly free. Off balance because she'd been straining to lean away, she hit the ground hard.

After that, everything happened so fast it was a blur. Delia crawled to a safe distance and watched the action unfold. Shaun was behaving like one of those actors in martial arts movies, only better! He struck the big man with one hand, then the other, and was out of reach before his opponent could return the first blow. He kicked high. He parried. He danced on the balls of his feet as if he were weightless. It was amazing! He was in perfect control of his body while his adversary threw useless punches that landed in thin air.

The heavier man hit the ground as a result of Shaun's sideways kick to his midsection and lay there, doubled up, his mouth opening and closing like that of a fish out of water.

Though she hadn't been counting the seconds, Delia guessed that her hero had won the battle in less than a minute. It was enough to take her breath away.

Delia accepted the hand Shaun offered and he pulled her to her feet.

"You okay?" he asked.

"Yes. Now," she managed. "Thanks."

When Shaun steadied her with an arm around her waist, she didn't object. Until then, she hadn't realized how wobbly she was.

"Who's your friend?" Shaun asked.

"I—I don't know."

"Then let's find out, shall we?" He rolled the thug over with a push of his boot. "What's your name?"

The answer came from between clenching teeth. "Erik Evans. I think you broke my ribs."

"Too bad," Shaun said. "Care to tell me what you were doing here?"

Evans glared at Delia. "I ain't got nothin' to say."

"Fine. Then we'll let the police figure it all out."

Shaun scooped up Delia's purse, retrieved her cell phone and handed it to her. "You in good enough shape to call them?"

She nodded and did as he'd asked, then handed the phone back to Shaun. The man on the ground had resumed a fetal position and was clearly no longer a threat. Realizing that, her body had apparently decided it was safe to shut down because without all that adrenaline coursing through her veins her exhaustion had returned.

Needing to draw on Shaun's strength as never before, she stepped up to him and slipped her arms around his waist. He pulled her close without hesitation.

She laid her cheek on his chest and listened to his rapid heartbeats. "I'm really glad to see you," she said softly. "Thanks again for coming to my rescue."

If she hadn't been in such close contact with him she might not have noticed that he took a shuddering breath before answering. "What were you doing here? Miranda said you'd gone back to Hawaii."

"I made a little detour first."

"So I see." Laying his cheek against her hair, Shaun took another deep breath. "Guess you caught this guy in the middle of a robbery."

Delia refused to lie to him. Instead, she merely held him tightly and tried to sort her confusion into useful thoughts. Shaun would probably understand the reasons for her change of plans if she explained them, but that didn't mean he'd keep the story to himself. After all, he didn't owe her any allegiance. Not anymore.

Sirens in the background heralded the arrival of the local police. They also roused the household and prompted Delia to reluctantly step away from Shaun.

Ronald, still in his bathrobe, was the first out the door. He was followed quickly by Juliet, Miranda and Aunt Winnie. In a third-floor window, Delia could see Peg, her grandfather's private nurse, peeking out and scowling with disapproval. Obviously, the sirens had provided a wake-up call for the entire household.

Everyone was peppering Delia with questions. She ignored the cacophony and briefly spoke to the two uniformed officers instead. They cuffed Erik Evans and strained to help him to his feet.

"I need an ambulance," the thug insisted, staggering.

"Yeah, buddy. We know. That young woman caught you casing the place and your pride is bruised, right?" The officers both laughed and started to guide him toward the patrol car.

Evans glared at Delia over his shoulder. "Lock me up and you'll be sorry. You'll never find out about the job," he warned.

Shivering, she felt Shaun's arm around her shoulders. If he was wondering what her attacker had meant, he was giving no outward indication of it. In a way, she wished he would quiz her about the man because she really needed to get the truth off her chest and Shaun had always been an easy person to talk to.

It would help to have another opinion, too. Perhaps Evans did have information she needed. Then again, maybe he'd been bluffing in the hope they'd drop the assault charges that were sure to result.

Either way, Delia knew she was going to have to confess sooner or later. Her conscience demanded it.

* * *

It was hours before the family calmed down enough to stop fussing over her. Delia had begged them to allow her to take a nap in the guest room on the second floor before discussing her reasons for being back in Maine and they had reluctantly agreed.

Ronald and Juliet had gone off to work at Blanchard Fabrics, Miranda was in her room as usual, Winnie was outside tending to her rose garden and Peg was upstairs with Grandfather Howard. That left only Shaun, who was supposed to be working in the library, patching the damage that had resulted from the shooting the month before.

Delia hoped he hadn't left when he'd realized she was still in residence because she really needed somebody sensible to talk to.

The moment she opened the door to the upstairs guest bedroom and started for the staircase she knew her unspoken prayers had been answered. She could hear the raspy sound of sanding from below.

Barefoot but still wearing jeans and a pink T-shirt, Delia tiptoed down the stairs. She slowly approached the entrance to the library, then gave Shaun her brightest smile when he glanced up and saw her.

"Hi," she said.

He'd taken one of the library doors off its hinges and placed it across a pair of sawhorses set atop a large tarp that protected the floor. He leaned over and continued to sand. "Hello."

"Did I thank you for saving my neck?"

"Over and over," Shaun said. He was still avoiding

her gaze but she was relieved to hear a smile in his tone.

She lounged against the doorjamb and crossed her arms. "So, where did you learn to fight like that?"

"In the army."

"No kidding? When were you in the army?"

"I enlisted after you went off to Hawaii."

"Ah." So much for innocent small talk. She supposed she and Shaun would always have trouble getting beyond their past. "Were you in the service a long time?"

"Long enough to pick up a few martial arts moves."

"Well, they sure came in handy this morning. Thanks."

Shaun chuckled cynically. "I believe you said that already."

"Yeah, I know. Words just seem inadequate for the situation. You saved my life, you know."

Shaun finally looked up from his work and smiled wryly. "I doubt that. The burglar was probably going to let you go any minute and run away to save himself from arrest. He'd already jammed the gate so it would stay open for his getaway. That's how I got in so easily."

"I—um—I don't think he was going to just let me go." The interest in Shaun's expression was enough to spur her to continue. "I didn't know his name, but that wasn't the first time I'd met Erik Evans."

Shaun put down the sandpaper, straightened and dusted off his hands. "Go on."

"Promise you won't say anything to my family?"

He nodded.

"Okay. Remember when everybody thought I was on my way to the airport to fly home? Well, I wasn't. I drove to upstate New York instead."

"That's what you meant when you said you took a detour? Why?" Shaun was listening carefully, his frown deepening.

"Well, because, there was this key in the stuff the coroner returned to us after the shooting and I thought somebody should check it out."

"One key?"

Delia nodded. "Yes. Just one. I know what you're thinking. I wondered myself why there wasn't a whole ring of keys, like to a car or whatever. Nobody knows how the victim got onto the estate grounds. I figured, if it really was Genie, the key I had might open her apartment, so…"

"You didn't!"

Delia took a step backward. "She was past caring. What harm could it do? I just wanted to find some clue to what had become of my mother and maybe get a sample of her sister's DNA."

"Did you?"

"No. I was so scared when that awful man showed up I completely forgot to take her hairbrush the way I'd planned."

"Speaking of Evans, what does he have to do with all this?"

"I don't know. That's the problem. He burst in while I was exploring Aunt Genie's place and

demanded money. He said he'd done some kind of
a job for her and she hadn't paid him. I can't see what
that can have to do with my mother, though."

"Maybe nothing," Shaun said thoughtfully. "But
the guy did hint that he knew something important.
If we don't try to make him talk, we'll never know."
He paused and drew his fingers over the point of his
chin. "I think you should tell your family."

Delia paled. "Everything?"

"Yes. Everything. I imagine your father's lawyers
can advise you how best to proceed. If Evans is as
stupid as he looks, it shouldn't be hard to get him to
open up to the right people." One eyebrow arched
over his steel-blue eyes. "And I don't mean *you*."

Icy wind blew onshore from the Atlantic with
ferocity, making the deserted Stoneley cemetery
seem even more forbidding. Moss-covered head-
stones stood in rows like silent sentinels guarding
their owners.

A solitary figure paused, shivering, at the foot of
the Blanchard family plot and glared at the mound
of recently turned earth that marked its newest grave.

*You're in the ground and still giving me trouble.
I should have known. Well, that can't be helped. It's
not as if I deprived the world of a useful citizen. I
don't know what all the fuss is about. You deserved
to die for what you did and you got exactly what was
coming to you. They should give me a medal.*

Ah, well, my time will come soon enough. Then

they'll all see and they can thank me. The ones who are on our side, that is. And the rest of them? It's not my fault if some of them are expendable. My darling will understand.

FOUR

Delia spent the remainder of the day dreading the angry confrontation she knew she'd face the minute she told her father the whole story. By the time Ronald came home from the office she'd gone over the details so often she just met him at the door and blurted them out.

Instead of the fury she'd expected, he reacted with astonishment. His ashen color worried her enough for her to lay a comforting hand on his sleeve. "Father?"

"I'm all right. Just surprised, that's all."

He shook off her touch and immediately headed for his study with Delia at his heels. As they passed the library, Shaun was picking up his tools. He fell in step beside Delia without hesitation.

"Did you tell him?" Shaun asked softly.

She nodded.

"What did he say?"

"Nothing, yet. Hush."

Ronald circled his massive desk, flipped through a Rolodex and started to punch buttons on the phone.

Delia and Shaun heard him speaking to someone who was obviously an attorney.

"That's right," Ronald said. "Erik Evans. He was picked up at the estate this morning and taken to jail in Stoneley. Have the charges against him dropped. If there's too much delay, bail him out. Immediately. I want a private meeting with him as soon as he's free. Arrange it."

He listened for a moment, then added, "No. This can't wait. I'll make time in my schedule."

Delia was no student of body language but she did find it rather off-putting that her father had cupped his hand tightly around the mouthpiece of the receiver, as if what he was saying wasn't being easily overheard by both her and Shaun.

When he hung up the phone he faced her. "It's taken care of. I'll meet with Evans as soon as he's released and find out what he knows. I can't imagine that anything Genie may have done which involved him was pertinent to us but we'll see." His smile was tight and seemed forced. "Will that satisfy you?"

What could Delia say under the circumstances? She nodded. "Yes. Thank you, Father."

Ronald looked to Shaun. "I suppose you're done with your work and want to be paid."

"Not quite," Shaun said. "The bullet splintered the wood when it exited and the repair was pretty extensive. It still needs at least one more coat of varnish. I should have the job done by tomorrow, though."

"Good. The sooner all reminders of that night are removed the better off we'll all be." He dismissed them with a wave of his hand. "Now, if you'll excuse me, I have a few more calls to make. In private."

Delia was embarrassed by the demeaning way her father had treated Shaun so she made a special effort to smooth things by walking out with him. "I'm sorry he was so abrupt," she said. "When God was passing out finesse my father must have been out to lunch."

"Better you should say it than me," Shaun replied with a half smile. "I never realized how hard it must have been growing up in a family with him as the patriarch."

"It had its moments," Delia said quietly. "My sisters and I all stuck together, as you know. And Aunt Winnie was wonderful. I don't know what we'd have done without her."

She smiled wistfully. "I remember lots of times when I wished Ian was my dad, instead. Your father is a sweet, sweet man." It was the first time in Delia's memory that she had voiced that sentiment and the stunned look on Shaun's face made her instantly wish she hadn't spoken so freely.

He quickly masked his feelings and changed the subject. "So, what are your plans now? Will you be flying home soon?"

"I suppose so. I have my own business to run and I need to get back to it. After Father speaks to Erik Evans and we find out what he wants to be paid for, I imagine that part of the mystery will be over."

"Probably," Shaun said.

"I wish I could stick around long enough to help

try to track down my mother but I'm afraid that could take years." Delia paused and sighed. "If we ever do find her."

"I'm glad you're being sensible for a change. There's no need to take any more chances. You've already gotten in way over your head."

His obvious concern was touching but his low opinion of her capabilities was a bit annoying. Instead of snapping at him, however, Delia chuckled.

"What's so funny?"

"You are," she said, continuing to be amused. "You don't have a clue about what I do for a living. You're a typical haole."

"What's that?"

"A foreigner. A nonnative Hawaiian. I compete in world-class surfing contests every year. I ride my board through the Pipeline off Oahu's North Shore and tackle thirty-foot waves for fun, not to mention all the times I'm paddling around in the ocean trying to teach novices how to do what I do without getting themselves hurt. If you think I take too many chances here in Maine, it's a good thing you haven't seen me surf!"

As Shaun paused at the library and turned away to pick up his toolbox she heard him murmur, "When you're right, you're right."

Shaun had spent another restless night and he was not happy about it. His life had been relatively uncomplicated until he'd returned to Stoneley. Now, it was anything but.

Worse, he couldn't just hit the road and escape the way he used to. His dad needed him. And he owed his father plenty. It was Ian who had listened for hours as he had unburdened his soul after he'd left the army and returned to the States to regroup. And it was Ian who had never passed judgment when Shaun had begun to wander all over the country in search of who-knows-what.

To Shaun's chagrin, seeing Delia again hadn't affected him the way he'd thought it would. He'd figured, now that he was older and seasoned by the curves life had thrown at him, he'd be immune to her charms. That was a laugh. If she'd stayed the immature, naive teen she'd been when they'd eloped, he could have dismissed her easily. The problem was, Delia had grown up, too. Boy, had she!

Oh, she looked about the same, with those big brown eyes and that silky hair of hers, although she'd cut it way too short to suit him. It was her heart and soul that had truly changed. Where she'd once been flighty, she was now focused. Where she'd once been easily swayed, she was now determined and strong-willed. The girl he had loved had grown into a formidable woman. A woman he couldn't help admiring immensely.

Shaun sighed as he climbed the front steps of Blanchard manor, hopefully for the last time. He'd be finished with the repairs to the door today and could start avoiding the place like the plague.

Although that conclusion should have pleased him, he felt a surprising sense of loss. What was wrong with him? He knew the answer instantly. Truth be told, he was going to miss seeing Delia, miss watching her quick mind work through the puzzles of her mother's disappearance, miss just being near her.

He knocked, waited a few seconds to no avail, then tried the door, found it unlocked and let himself in. The Blanchards were expecting him so it was unlikely anyone would mistake him for a prowler. Then again, he was there to finish repairing a bullet hole that had splintered their fancy woodwork. No telling what could happen in this house.

His mind zeroed in on Delia once again. The sooner she left Stoneley and went back to Hawaii where she'd be safe, the better he'd feel about this whole situation. Like it or not, he desperately wanted to continue to protect her.

Making his way quietly down the hall, Shaun went to work. One more fine sanding and a last, thin coat of varnish and the inlaid door would be good as new.

He huffed derisively. He wished he could say the same for his psyche. His scars were a lot more than skin-deep.

A man's voice echoed down the hall from the study. Ronald Blanchard was either talking to himself or speaking on the telephone. Shaun didn't want to listen to the other man's conversation but he couldn't help overhearing.

"I need to talk to somebody, get this business off my chest, work some things out," Ronald was saying. "No. Not on the phone. In person. When will you be available?"

At first, Shaun assumed Delia's father was referring to his upcoming meeting with his lawyers and Erik Evans. Then, Ronald said, "Fine. Your office at Unity, 10:00 a.m. today. I'll be there."

Wind from a hummingbird's wings could have blown Shaun over! It sounded as if the usually oh-so-perfect, overbearing Ronald Blanchard had just made a counseling appointment with Greg Brown, the pastor of Unity Christian Church! Miracles *did* still happen these days. Apparently, learning that he'd buried the wrong person and that his ex-wife was probably still alive had shaken old Ronald to the core. Well, good. If ever a man deserved to have a spasm of conscience, that one did. Too bad it had come too late to help him and Delia.

Shaun gritted his teeth. There they were again. Thoughts of Delia. They refused to leave him alone no matter how hard he tried to banish them. He could still feel the touch of her hand when he'd held it in front of the police station; still sense the warmth of her embrace when he'd come to her rescue on the front lawn of the mansion and she'd stepped into his arms as if it were the most natural thing in the world.

"I've probably been sniffing too many solvent fumes," he mumbled to himself. "I mean, it's not like we ever had a real chance together. We were too different."

He pretended not to notice when Ronald passed outside in the hallway and cast a condescending

glance in his direction. The man's pettiness was unbelievable. If he hadn't been Delia's father, Shaun
would have considered the whole incident little more
than an amusing footnote to a trying job. A job that,
thankfully, was nearly over.

Delia smelled the fresh varnish, assumed it meant
that Shaun was in the house and came to investigate.
Relieved to find she was right, she greeted him with
a smile. "Morning."

"Good morning." He didn't look up. "Can't stop
now. One second and I'll have this coat finished."

She lingered, thumbs hooked into the front
pockets of her jeans. "Don't let me disturb you."

"You're not. I just need to keep the brushstrokes
going with the grain so they don't show when it's
dry."

Delia laughed lightly. "Good thing you've never
seen me paint. I used a big, fuzzy roller to do the
outside of my surf shop in a really bright blue. It
looked great. But by the time I was done I had more
paint on me and the ground than I did on the wall."

"No doubt." Shaun straightened and carefully
dipped the brush into a shallow container of mineral
spirits to clean it. "You don't seem to tackle
anything halfway."

"I'll take that as a compliment." She was delighted to see a grin spreading across his face and
crinkling the corners of his eyes.

"It was meant to be," he said, methodically wiping
the bristles on a clean rag. "So, are you all packed?"

"I never unpacked from my last adventure," Delia said. "As soon as Father has had his meeting with that awful thug that followed me from Aunt Genie's, I'm history." She eyed the den. "I thought I heard him down here."

"He was. He just left."

"Oh." Delia couldn't help feeling relieved. "Well, no problem. I'm sure he'll tell me what he finds out."

Shaun raised an eyebrow. "Are you?"

"Of course. Why wouldn't he?"

"I don't know. Maybe because you have a habit of taking matters into your own hands? I'd have to think twice before I gave you any encouragement to get more involved. I imagine your father feels the same way."

"I only act if nobody else is doing anything," she insisted. "Sometimes I feel as though I'm the only one in the ocean who sees the sharks circling. Know what I mean?"

"Not exactly. But I think I get the general idea and it scares me."

"I'm not reckless, if that's what you mean. I just don't have a lot of patience."

Shaun gave her a lopsided smile. "I was referring to the part about the sharks. Do you see lots of those in your line of work?"

"A few. Jellyfish are far more likely to hurt you. Sharks are usually not dangerous."

He shook his head as though he thought she was seriously deluded. "*Usually* not dangerous?"

"Hey, no job is without its hazards. Take your stint in the army, for instance. Where did they send you? What did you do?"

To her dismay, Shaun's countenance darkened and his eyes narrowed. "I'd rather not talk about it."

"Okay. Fine. What would you like to talk about?"

"Nothing. I'm almost finished here. I'll be out of your hair as soon as this door is dry enough to rehang."

Delia pulled a face. She was still searching for a snappy retort and coming up blank when the extension phone in the library began to ring. Since it was closer than the one in her father's study she sidled past Shaun and lifted the receiver.

"Blanchard residence." She cocked her head as she listened to the caller and looked back at Shaun. "No. I understand my father has gone out."

Shaun nodded.

"Yes. That's right. I believe he left a few minutes ago. Why?" She paused, listening. Her breathing grew more rapid. Staring at Shaun, she continued her conversation but she knew there was no way she could hide her astonishment and concern so she didn't try.

Finally, she said, "Yes. Yes, I'll tell him. Thank you for calling."

Shaun's eyes were asking countless questions. Delia propped a hip against the edge of the heavy library table to steady herself before she said, "We have a problem."

Shaun was beside her in two long strides. "What happened? You look like you've seen a ghost."

"I should be so lucky," she gibed, wanting to lighten the subject yet knowing it was beyond serious, at least where she and her family were concerned. "It's Erik Evans. Right after Father's lawyer got him out of jail, the guy disappeared."

"How is that possible?"

"I don't know. The man's a career criminal. I'm sure he knows lots of tricks of the trade. After all, he managed to follow me back here after I did everything I could to be sure I was in the clear."

"The police will find him."

Delia shook her head. "No, they won't. The charges were officially dropped, just like Father wanted. Nobody cares where Evans went. Nobody except the Blanchards."

The intense concentration on Shaun's face reminded her of the way he'd looked when he'd been battling to free her from the thug's clutches the day before.

"We have to tell your father what's happened," Shaun said. "Until we're sure Evans is long gone, he could be dangerous."

Delia gripped his muscular forearm, immediately mindful of the inappropriateness of her actions yet unwilling to let go right away and deprive herself of the strong sense of Shaun's support. "You think Father may be in danger?"

"I don't know. Do you have his cell phone number?"

"Yes. I'll call him right away."

She punched in the numbers and listened to the

recorded message, then explained, "The service says he's unavailable. He must have shut off his phone for some reason."

"I can understand why," Shaun said. He took her elbow and steered her toward the door. "Grab your purse and come on. I'll drive. I'm pretty sure I know where he is."

Ronald Blanchard was disgusted with himself. Here he was, a captain of industry, arguably Stoneley's leading citizen, and yet he felt just like a naughty schoolboy entering the principal's office.

He squared his shoulders beneath his finely tailored suit coat, straightened his silk tie and pushed open the exterior door to the historic Unity Christian Church. He knew where Greg Brown's office was. The problem was, he'd never come there for anything resembling counseling before. The idea of needing anyone's advice, especially that of a much younger man, galled him enough that he almost turned and left.

Thankfully, Brown's secretary was away from her desk when Ronald arrived and he was able to proceed directly into the private section of the office.

The pastor's warm brown eyes reflected compassion and genuine concern as he rose and extended his hand. "Good to see you, Mr. Blanchard. How can I help you?"

Ronald shook his hand firmly. "I'm not sure you can. I'm not even sure why I'm here. The notion of talking to someone who can be totally objective kept nagging at me and I thought..."

"Of course. Please, have a seat." The pastor circled his desk, gestured at a pair of occasional chairs and waited for Ronald to choose one before he settled into the other. "What's on your mind?"

"That's a good question," Ronald said, sighing. "I guess it's mostly women."

A smile lifted the corners of Pastor Greg's mouth and made his eyes sparkle. "You couldn't have picked a tougher subject."

Beginning to relax in the man's pleasant company, Ronald returned his smile. "I supposed not. I wish they were as easy to understand as a spreadsheet or an auditor's report."

Pastor Greg chuckled. "That'll be the day."

"I imagine so. Actually, my problem seems to be that I'm still in love with my ex-wife." Incredulous, even though he knew his words to be the truth, he shook his head. "Maybe I'd better slow down, go back and start my story at the beginning so you'll know what I'm talking about."

The pastor nodded. "Take your time. I'm listening."

"Why won't you tell me where we're going?" Delia was seated beside Shaun in the Murphy Woodworkers' truck and watching the familiar, historically significant buildings of Stoneley pass in a blur.

"Because I'm not sure I'm right. I see no need to stir things up worse than they already are."

"As if you could." She pulled a face. "If things get any more complicated I think I'll scream."

"Please don't. My reputation is already shaky

enough." His gaze met Delia's and she had to smile in return.

Shaun slowed the truck and started to pull into the parking lot of Unity Christian Church. Delia was positive he was making a mistake until she spotted her father's sleek, black town car parked beside the modest silver SUV of the pastor, Greg Brown.

"My father is *here?*"

Shaun nodded and parked. "Looks like it."

"How did you know?"

"I overheard him making the appointment. I was trying so hard to keep from listening, I was afraid I might have been mistaken. That's why I didn't want to say anything till we'd seen for sure. It seemed totally out of character for Ronald to seek counseling."

"Boy, that's an understatement. Maybe finding out that my mother may still be alive shook him up more than I thought."

"Maybe. Do you want me to go in with you?"

"Uh-uh. As long as he's with the pastor he's safe enough. Would you mind if we just sat here and waited for him to come out?"

Shaun shrugged. "Fine by me. I charge by the job, not by the hour, and I don't have anything else lined up. Folks in Stoneley apparently heard how sick Dad was, assumed he couldn't work and stopped calling. Business has been terrible lately."

"I am sorry. I'm glad Miranda thought of you—I mean of Ian—when we needed your expertise. You did a beautiful job on that door. I didn't think it could be fixed so well with all those splinters on the back."

"Bullets can do that. They make a little hole going in, then tear things up pretty badly on the way out."

"I suppose you did a lot of shooting when you were in the service." The minute the words were out of her mouth she knew how ridiculous the question was. The look on Shaun's face told her he agreed.

He shrugged. "Naw. We used snowballs and baseball bats." He chuckled wryly. "Yes, Delia, they gave me a gun. And I learned to use it effectively. Now, can we talk about something else?"

"Like what?"

"Beats me." He settled back, still behind the wheel, with his arms folded across his chest. "Why don't you tell me about Hawaii?"

She sighed and nodded. "Oh, I'd *love* to. I hardly know where to start. I live on the North Shore of Oahu near Ehukai Beach Park. That's where the Triple Crown surfing events take place in November and December. Lots of people come there to watch us surf the Banzai Pipeline, even when we're not competing." She grinned at him. "We get phenomenal waves every winter at Ehukai and next door at Sunset Beach."

"I think I've heard of the Pipeline."

"I'm not surprised. It's world famous. In the summer, the waves on the North Shore die down and the best action moves to the south. I take my students to whichever beach best fits their capabilities."

Delia gave a little shiver in spite of the sunlight

streaming in the truck's windows. "And it's warm there. So warm. Balmy and beautiful almost all the time."

"You don't miss the four seasons?"

"We have seasons," she said, "Summer, summer, summer and rainy summer. "If I want to freeze to death just going to the grocery store, I can always come back here to visit. Actually, I try to make it back most years for Aunt Winnie's birthday party and the Winter Fest. The most important surfing competitions are over by then."

She took a deep, settling breath, releasing it as a quiet sigh. "Thanks to the problems surrounding my family, I think I've accumulated more frequent-flier miles in the last few months than most people rack up in years."

"I'm sorry."

"Thanks." She gave him her most amiable smile and was rewarded with one of his heart-stopping grins. That was enough incentive to cause her to reach over and squeeze his hand for a brief moment.

Shaun cleared his throat and looked as though he was about to say something important, but the moment was broken when she saw her father leaving the church by a side door. Pastor Greg Brown had followed him. The men were shaking hands when Delia approached.

"Father! I'm glad I caught you. Hello, Pastor Greg."

Both men acknowledged her. Ronald looked as if he wished a chasm would open in the pavement and swallow him. "Delia. What are you doing here?"

"I came to find you. To warn you," she explained without hesitation. "Your attorney's office called."

"And?"

Delia glanced at the pastor, then focused on her father. She knew Ronald didn't like airing their family's dirty laundry but since he had asked, she felt comfortable answering directly.

"Erik Evans has skipped town. They don't know where he went after they got him out of jail and they thought you should know."

Ronald started to curse, then apparently thought better of it considering the company he was presently keeping and stopped. "All right." He scanned the parking lot and spotted Shaun. "I see you used your head for once and didn't come alone. Have Murphy take you back to the house and tell him to stay there until I get home. I have one stop to make first."

"At the office?"

Her father shook his head. His eyes met the warm, understanding gaze of the young pastor. "No. I've decided to break off my relationship with Alannah Stafford and I think I owe it to her to do it in person."

Delia couldn't help registering the shock she was feeling. "You are? You do? What happened?"

"I've been talking to Pastor Greg about my feelings for Trudy," Ronald said. "We agree that it's unfair to Alannah to keep up the pretense that there's a chance for us as a couple when I know there isn't."

"Wow." Delia blinked, trying to take it all in. Her father had appeared to be head over heels in love with Alannah, had given the woman expensive furs and jewelry and who knows what else, and now he was planning to break up with her? It was unbelievable!

It was also the right thing to do, but since when had Ronald Blanchard developed a conscience?

FIVE

Shaun had finished rehanging the recently repaired door by the time Ronald arrived at the mansion.

Delia left Shaun gathering up the last of his supplies and met her father at the front door. "I'm so glad you're finally here. How did it go?"

He huffed. "Not terribly well."

"I'm sorry. Was she furious?"

"That's an understatement. I suppose I should have expected it. She threatened to make me rue the day we met. She's a little late. I already do." He snorted cynically. "She threatened to get even with me—with my family—to make us pay."

"What did you say then?"

"I told her she'd have to take a number and get in line. Funny. When she was ranting and raving at me she wasn't a bit beautiful. It was as if her mask had slipped and let me see the real Alannah beneath the superficial facade. I don't know what attracted me to her in the first place."

Delia could have listed many possibilities, not

the least of which was the other woman's model-perfect appearance and sophisticated demeanor, but she chose to hold her tongue. They had worse problems than coping with her father's angry ex-girlfriend. They still had Erik Evans's whereabouts to consider.

"Let's go discuss this where the servants can't overhear us," she said. "I have an idea."

Ronald shook his head. "No. Leave Alannah to me."

"Gladly," Delia said. "I don't intend to give her another thought. What I want to talk about is finding Evans."

"I'll put private detectives on the case. They'll locate him."

Shepherding her father past the open library doors she made eye contact with Shaun to let him know she wanted him to accompany them. Together, the three entered Ronald's study across the wide hallway. The room had a mannish, somber tone with its dark, burnished wood and leather furnishings and Ronald's massive yet elegant desk.

Delia closed the door for privacy while her father circled the desk and settled into his swivel chair.

She turned to face him boldly. "I want to go looking for Evans myself."

Before her father spoke she could read his negative reaction in his body language and harsh expression.

"Nonsense."

"It's not anything of the kind," Delia countered.

"It's sensible. He's already met me. He's far more likely to tell me what's been going on than he is to blab as the result of strong-arm tactics."

Ronald eyed Shaun. "Oh, I don't know. He seemed pretty impressed after Murphy got through with him."

"Never mind that," Delia said. "Let me put it another way. I'm going after Evans. Period. Whether you give me your blessing or not."

Ronald's face reddened. "No. You are *not*."

"Oh?"

"Delia, be sensible. You don't even know where this man lives. Granted, you're smart, but you're no detective. Let the professionals handle it. That's what I pay them for."

"You can hire a dozen private investigators. A hundred. That won't change how I feel." She placed her palms flat on the desk opposite her father, and stared him down. "I'm going."

Frowning, his jaw set, Ronald glanced across the room and made eye contact with Shaun. "Can't you talk some sense into her?"

"Me?" Shaun snorted cynically. "Not likely."

The older man's shoulders slumped and he leaned back in his leather chair, looking every one of his nearly sixty years. "Unfortunately, that's partly my fault," Ronald said broodingly, "and if it's any consolation at this late date, I'm sorry, Murphy."

Delia thought she must be imagining things. It almost sounded as if her father was apologizing to Shaun! Her head snapped around, her gaze locking with Shaun's. Judging by the astonishment on his handsome face, he'd gotten the same impression. What an extraordinary development. If she hadn't heard it with her own ears she wouldn't have believed it.

"Look," Ronald said, still concentrating on Shaun, "I know this isn't your fight but I also know there's no one else who can handle my headstrong daughter the way you can. Would you be willing to stick with her? See that she doesn't get hurt?"

Shaun scowled. "What makes you think she'll listen to me any better than she listens to anybody else?"

"I don't know that she will," Ronald said. "But I'll feel a lot better knowing you're backing her up."

"Well…"

Delia had heard enough. "Hold it. Just hold it. You two are discussing me as though I'm not standing right here in front of you. Don't I have some say in all this?"

To her astonishment, Shaun and Ronald uttered a simultaneous, *"No!"*

Hours later, Delia was upstairs in the second floor guest room, muttering to herself over what had transpired in the study and trying to control her emotional reactions to it. She was thunderstruck. Shaun Murphy and Ronald Blanchard, sworn adversaries, had made their peace and had teamed up to thwart her. Never in her wildest dreams had she imagined anything like that would ever take place. She didn't know which felt worse—bucking her father's usually unquestioned authority or winning the argument only if Shaun's continued presence was part of her victory. Some victory!

She was no fool. She knew that her father had only given in because he expected his hired investigators to reach Erik Evans long before she did. They very well might. That didn't keep her from wanting—from needing—to do something besides sit around and twiddle her thumbs while her family was going through a hypothetical tempest.

Thoughtful, Delia walked to the window and looked down on the spacious estate grounds. Spring was in full bloom below, thanks to the ministrations of the groundskeepers and the special touches Aunt Winnie gave to her rose garden. Daffodils had faded but there were lush beds of lavender and blue pansies at the feet of tree peonies that would soon be heavy with pink-and-white blooms the size of grapefruits. The dark green and deep reds and purples of groupings of rhododendrons provided the perfect contrast. The grass had greened up nicely after the last snow of early spring, too, and was cut and edged so precisely it looked like green velvet from her upstairs vantage point.

She wrapped her arms around herself and sighed. How could such a beautiful place feel so cold, so bleak, so uninviting? No matter how elegant the decor, no matter how delectable the food, no matter how welcoming the greetings from her aunt and sisters, Delia simply could not feel at home in Blanchard manor.

She didn't know exactly when her alienation had come to fruition but she knew when it had begun. The day her father had permanently ruined her marriage was the day she had closed her heart to anything pertaining to him or his lifestyle.

She turned away from the window. "I shouldn't be thinking of myself," she muttered. "The past is beyond repair and there's much more at stake here than whatever happiness I may have lost." Her lips curled into a self-deprecating smile and made her chuckle. "Hey, when I'm right, I'm right. I just wish other people realized how smart I am."

But was she smart enough, Delia wondered, to figure out exactly what was going on? There was such a tangled web of lies surrounding her mother's sad, wasted life she wondered if anyone would ever learn the whole truth. Maybe it shouldn't matter at this late date. Then again, maybe it mattered more now than ever. If Trudy was alive, and if Genie had somehow been involved in the convoluted mysteries surrounding her family, there might be a chance that Erik Evans had some critical answers. The only way to find out was to track him down and make him talk.

Pacing the floor of the guest room and mumbling to herself was getting Delia nowhere. Grabbing her cell phone she punched in the number for Murphy Woodworkers without conscious thought, then felt her heart speed when she realized what she'd done.

Wow! That was scary. Apparently, her memory had retained Shaun's old number from the days when she'd telephoned him constantly just to hear his deep, nerve-tingling voice. Truth to tell, she was every bit as eager to do so right now.

When Ian answered, Delia pushed aside her disappointment and greeted him pleasantly. "Hello, Mr. Murphy. This is Delia Blanchard. I hate to bother you. May I please speak to Shaun?"

"Good to hear from you, Delia," the older man said. "How have you been?"

"Fine, thanks. I was sorry to hear that you haven't been well."

Ian chuckled. "Getting old isn't for sissies. Hang on. Shaun's around here somewhere. I'll get him."

In seconds, the voice she had longed to hear said, "Hello?"

Delia gripped the little phone more tightly. "Shaun?" Though she'd intended to come across as calm and collected, her anxiety immediately pushed to the forefront. "What's taking you so long? I figured you'd call when you were ready to go so I could pick you up."

"You aren't actually serious about us hitting the road together, are you?"

"Of course I am. Why shouldn't I be?" She heard unintelligible muttering on the other end of the line before Shaun's clear, "Yes, Dad, I know, but…"

"We'll only be gone a few days at the most," she reminded him. "My father said he'd compensate you as if you were working so you can assure Ian that your absence won't hurt a thing."

"I already did."

"Then what's the problem? The longer we delay, the less likely we'll catch up to Evans."

"Do you honestly think you and I have a chance to succeed? Think about it, Delia. We're novices. Even with the address you got from your father's lawyers, our chances of finding the guy are slim to none. New York's a big state. Besides, what makes you think he'd go back to his old neighborhood? If I were him, I wouldn't."

"You wouldn't because you're intelligent," she said. "I hate to be judgmental but I don't think Erik Evans is too bright."

"That doesn't mean he isn't crafty. Even wild animals are smart enough to avoid traps."

"True, assuming there isn't a bigger picture that we're not seeing."

"What do you mean?"

Delia paused, deciding to speak her mind. "I've been giving this whole messed-up situation a lot of thought, Shaun. Suppose I was meant to run into Evans at Aunt Genie's the way I did? And suppose your work at the house was delayed just so you'd be there to rescue me from him? The whole chain of events seems pretty far-fetched otherwise."

"Coincidence. Things like that happen all the time."

"Not to me, they don't. I've only recently realized that learning about my mother's fate was the answer to my prayers. Very *old* prayers but prayers, just the same. I'm beginning to think I only glimpsed a hint of the answer that's coming. Maybe all these other things are part of a larger whole."

"Are you trying to tell me you see the hand of *God* in all this?"

"Maybe. Maybe not. I'm keeping an open mind. The way I see it, anything that makes my father admit his mistakes and brings him to Pastor Greg for counseling has to border on the miraculous."

"Now *there,* we agree." Shaun paused and blew out a noisy breath. "Okay. It won't take me long to throw a few things into a duffel bag and hit the ATM."

The notion of spending the night near Shaun, even though she knew they wouldn't actually be together, gave Delia the kind of tickly shivers she got just before tackling a dangerous wave.

"Don't worry about expenses," she told him. "We'll have Father's credit card for gas and lodging so we'll be able to afford nice rooms."

She heard him coughing for a few seconds before he managed an insistent, "*Separate* rooms."

"Of course. What did you think?"

Shaun cleared his throat. "Believe me, Delia," he said hoarsely, "you don't want to know the half of what I think."

She's leaving town. Good. The less I have to do with her the better. She's a smart one. Clever. Too clever. The next thing you know she'll be asking questions about things that are none of her business. Private things. Special things that are mine, alone. He listens to her too much. Lets her get away with treating him disrespectfully. That can't be tolerated. It simply will not do. I won't allow it.

But first things first. While Delia's gone and can't interfere, can't spoil it, there's something I need to take care of.

With a snide smile the plotter added, *Later I'll deal with little Delia. She may think she has the upper hand but she won't win. I've been patient so far. I can wait. I'll take care of her in due time.*

Shaun was surprised when Delia arrived at the cabinet shop in her father's sleek, black SUV instead of her rental car. He was even more surprised when she deferred to him and changed seats to let him drive.

"This is quite a vehicle," he said, fastening his shoulder belt.

"Taking it was my father's idea. I refused to accept one of the town cars so he insisted we use this."

"It's substantial. That's good. The car you've been driving is pretty wimpy in comparison."

He was thinking of defensive driving. When Delia didn't seem to catch on, he dropped the subject. It was just as well that she wasn't aware of her obvious vulnerability the way he and her father were. That was why he had agreed to accompany her on this wild-goose chase. Delia needed watching, protecting, and he was just the man to do it.

Shaun smiled to himself. She'd be indignant if she suspected how fragile he thought she was. Yes, she was strong and athletic, for a woman, but she was still female and therefore no physical match for a man, let alone one as burly as Erik Evans. Even if the guy fought fair, which wasn't likely, he could easily overpower Delia. The notion of her becoming Evans's victim turned Shaun's stomach and made him grip the steering wheel so tightly his knuckles whitened.

"Are you okay?" she asked.

"Fine. Why?"

Her laugh echoed inside the SUV. "Because you're holding that wheel like you're trying to strangle it. If I didn't trust you, I wouldn't have given you the keys. Relax. I know you're a good driver."

Memory tied Shaun's gut in an even bigger knot. It wasn't Delia's fault, of course. She couldn't possibly suspect why her innocent praise had cut so deeply. Nobody but Ian knew the whole story and he'd never have told anyone else, least of all Delia.

Still, her comment stung. Good driver? Sure. Tell that to his buddies, especially the ones who hadn't made it back to the barracks after…

Shaun gritted his teeth and tried to force remembrances of that life-changing night to the back of his mind. He'd been over and over the details, always hoping he'd find a way to excuse himself. He never had. Everybody made mistakes. It just wasn't every mistake that cost people's lives the way his had.

Friends weren't the only things he'd lost on those night maneuvers. Shaun had lain in the wreckage of the personnel carrier, covered with mud and the blood of his hurt and dying comrades, and had prayed for their deliverance with all his heart. He had lived, yes, but not all of the others had.

Army docs had insisted he was merely suffering from survivor's guilt and would recover. Well, Delia could pretend all she wanted that a benevolent Heavenly Father cared what happened on Earth. Shaun knew better. He had buried his faith with his friends. It wasn't himself he no longer trusted. It was God.

Delia forced herself to keep quiet while Shaun brooded. She'd seen him do it before and recognized the signs. This time, however, she was totally at a loss to figure out what had triggered his moodiness. It couldn't be their situation. As far as she could tell, he had accepted their bizarre reasons for banding together pretty well.

That thought almost made her smile in spite of her companion's dour expression. Whatever Shaun's feelings were, they *had* to be more settled than hers. Being this close to him for hours had left her as uneasy as if she had accidentally waded into a floating school of poisonous jellyfish. The likelihood of stinging, lingering pain was great in either situation and the longer she stayed, the greater the risk. Like her emotions, the gelatinous creatures drifted just below the surface, unseen but definitely a presence to be reckoned with.

Finally, she decided to try to improve Shaun's mood, for her own sake as much as his. "So," she said brightly, "are we there yet?"

He cast her a sullen look. "Not hardly."

"That's what I figured. Mind if I call home and

check with Aunt Winnie to see if she's heard anything? There's no point continuing if Father's fancy detectives have already located Evans."

"Why ask me? I'm just your bodyguard, remember?"

"Point taken—grumpy." Delia pushed the speed dial on her cell phone and plugged her opposite ear with a fingertip while she listened to the ringing.

To her surprise, her eldest sister answered with an uncharacteristically breathless, "Hello?"

"Miranda?"

"Oh, Delia, I'm so glad you called! Something terrible has happened."

"What's wrong? You sound awful." As she spoke she made eye contact with Shaun and answered his quizzical look with an arch of her brow and a quick shrug. "It's not Aunt Winnie, is it? Tell me she's okay."

"She's fine," Miranda said. "Grandfather Howard had some kind of spell. We thought he was going to die. Peg gave him first aid while we waited for the paramedics."

"Are they still there?"

"No. Everybody followed the ambulance to the hospital. Except Peg, that is. She rode with Grandfather."

To Delia's relief, Shaun had pulled the SUV to the curb and stopped. She got out to pace the sidewalk while she spoke with Miranda. Shaun joined her.

"Peg's been his nurse for ages," Delia said, frowning. "She should know what was wrong with him. What did she say?"

"Nothing. She looked as worried as the rest of us. It was so frightening. He was breathing hard and sweating and shaking all over. I heard one of the paramedics say Grandfather's heart was racing and I think he passed out right after that happened."

Those symptoms reminded Delia of her sister's tendency toward panic attacks and she didn't want her questions to further agitate Miranda and push her past the limits of her own self-control. "So, we know he's in good hands now," Delia said soothingly. "How are *you* doing?"

"I'm still a little shaky, but who wouldn't be, under the circumstances?" She sighed. "I'm just glad you were spared witnessing Grandfather's collapse."

Delia smiled to herself. It was just like Miranda to want to protect her younger siblings from anything traumatic. "How long ago did all this trouble start?"

"It had to be around one o'clock. Barbara Sanchez had stopped by to have lunch with Father, Aunt Winnie and me. After Sonya had finished serving our main course, she went upstairs to take Grandfather his usual cup of tea and found him in distress. That's all I know."

"Where was Peg? She's supposed to watch him."

"We can't expect her to sit with him every second," Miranda said. "I think she was having lunch in the kitchen with Sonya."

Delia checked her watch. "Okay. I imagine it will be a while longer before the doctors know anything. I'll check with the hospital and see. Do you have the number handy?" She motioned to Shaun and he produced a pen and paper.

Delia jotted down the number of Stoneley Memorial Hospital, then said, "Got it. Okay. I'll call later and get a report."

Actually, call me on my cell," Miranda said. "We should probably keep this line free in case somebody else wants to get in touch with me."

Delia let out a deep, shuddering breath. "This is just so awful."

"It was. But there are some things we can't change. Grandfather's condition has been getting worse and worse lately, in spite of the best medical treatment money can buy. We have to accept that. And remember, Grandfather is in God's hands."

"You're right. It's just hard to imagine this house without him upstairs, cursing and ranting all the time." Delia paused. "I'm sorry. I shouldn't have said that. I know he can't help what the Alzheimer's disease is doing to his mind and body."

"No more than the rest of us can help our natural reactions to the cruel things he says and does," Miranda concurred.

Delia's thoughts were whirling. "Tell everybody I'll be home as soon as possible. And in case no one else has done it, why don't you notify Pastor Greg? He'll want to know. Ask him to start the prayer chain, too."

"I should have thought of that," her sister said, clearly berating herself for the oversight.

"With all the excitement, it's a wonder I did."

Delia bade her sister a fond goodbye and flipped the little phone closed before she looked at Shaun. His expression was unreadable, particularly because he had donned reflective sunglasses that hid his eyes.

"I take it Howard is ill," he said, starting to place his arm around her shoulders then hesitating as if he'd suddenly changed his mind.

"Yes. He's apparently having some kind of health crisis. They've taken him to the hospital in an ambulance."

"I'm sorry. Something else seems to be weighing on you. Want to talk about it?"

She decided she did. Very much. "I just can't help thinking what a waste his life has been." She sniffled in spite of her determination to remain emotionally in control. "It's so sad."

"Howard Blanchard's life was wasted? I doubt many people would agree with you there. He built a thriving business and your father is continuing to expand it. Most folks envy them."

Delia raised her gaze to meet and hold his, willing him to understand what she was just beginning to grasp, herself. "The success of Blanchard Fabrics has nothing to do with it, except maybe where it warped their personalities and skewed their values," Delia said. "He and my father are two of the most miserable men I've ever known. They may have more money than they know what to do with but they haven't a clue about what's really important."

"I imagine they'd both disagree with you."

"Undoubtedly. But, 'All that glisters is not gold.'"

"Shakespeare?"

"Of course. *Merchant of Venice.* I think what it means is what I was trying to explain. A lot of things that seem important and worthwhile may be utterly superficial. My family's money is like that. Father and Grandfather have never understood that the love of their family, for instance, is worth far more than whatever they gained from all that time they spent at work. They virtually ignored everybody else. I don't know what my sisters and I would have done without Aunt Winnie's love and moral support."

Shaun gave her hand a brief squeeze and Delia returned the gesture, grieving for her grandfather in her own way.

"I'd forgotten how you always seem to have a Shakespearian quote for every occasion," he said fondly.

"Umm. I suppose you're right."

Thankful beyond words for Shaun's support when she was battling such mixed emotions, Delia stepped into his embrace, closed her eyes and laid her cheek on his chest. She could hear the strong beating of his heart and his even breathing. If she could have stood there, sheltered in Shaun's arms, for hours and hours she would have.

When her subconscious suddenly dredged up a meaningful scripture from the fifth chapter of The Song of Solomon instead of the usual snippet of Shakespeare, she wisely chose to keep the biblical quotation to herself.

Reveling in Shaun's closeness, she marveled at how the deepest reaches of her mind had revealed what she had been denying for twelve years.

"This is my beloved, and this is my friend," she quoted silently, over and over. She sighed. Like it or not, that was the absolute truth and always would be.

SIX

Later calls to Stoneley Memorial Hospital and to Miranda provided little new information. Howard Blanchard had been stabilized, admitted to the hospital and was undergoing a battery of tests. Beyond that, his doctors had nothing to relate except that he was resting comfortably and seemed to be out of danger for the present.

That was one of the reasons Delia had chosen to press on in spite of Shaun's suggestion that they return to Stoneley instead.

"There's nothing I can do back in Maine but sit around the hospital waiting room with the others and wring my hands," Delia explained. "Miranda says Grandfather is sedated, anyway. There's absolutely no reason for us to race back there."

"Are you sure that's what you want to do?" he asked.

She pressed her lips together in a thin line. "Yes. I suppose you think it's awful of me but please remember, he doesn't know us half the time, anyway.

And the times when he is lucid, he's an evil, nasty old man. I can't believe the horrid things he said to Juliet when he mistook her for our mother. He was so furious and out of control I thought he was actually going to hit her."

"I heard plenty about Howard when he was younger," Shaun said. "I don't doubt that his illness has sharpened his temper." He reached across the SUV and laid his hand over Delia's. "I just don't want you to have any regrets if he doesn't make it."

She managed a smile while she blinked back unshed tears. "Knowing me, I'd have regrets no matter what I did or didn't do. It seems like I'm always trying to second-guess God. I'm afraid I don't get it right very often."

Giving her hand a parting pat he concentrated on the road ahead without further comment. On the dashboard, the GPS map was flashing. "Looks like we're pretty close," he said, pointing. "Another five miles or so to the turnoff."

"I know. I…" Delia frowned and studied the passing side streets. "This whole area seems very familiar. Let's get off early."

"The map says to stay on Eighty-seven."

"I know, but I have a feeling we're only a little ways from where Aunt Genie used to live and I have this odd urge to drive by her place and have another look. Maybe get the DNA I forgot the first time." She pointed. "Over there. Take that road."

"Okay. You're the boss."

Delia laughed softly. "That'll be the day. I can't believe how you and my father got together just to boss me around. You both act like you think I'm *lolo*."

Shaun's eyebrows arched. "Is that Hawaiian for *stupid?*"

"How'd you guess?" She made a sardonic face. "I wouldn't have believed it if I hadn't seen it with my own eyes. You and Father have never agreed on a single thing, until now."

"We're both concerned about your well-being, that's all," Shaun said. He'd done as she'd asked, slowed the SUV on the surface streets, and was leaning forward to peer out the windshield. "Does any of this look familiar to you?"

She noted the carefully tended lawns with their artistically arching specimen trees and too-perfect arrangements of shrubs. "I think so."

"Well, it sure isn't the kind of neighborhood I imagine Evans lives in."

"No, but it seems right for Aunt Genie. I wish I'd remembered to bring her address. So many of these upscale condominium complexes along the lake look alike."

Her breath caught. She pointed again. "Look! Over there. See that black motorcycle parked in the cul-de-sac? Do you suppose…?"

Shaun immediately wheeled in and parked parallel to the curb. "Yeah. I do." He shut off the motor and set the emergency brake. "Stay here."

She had already hopped out of the car and was

headed toward the nearest buildings before his feet hit the ground.

"No way," she called over her shoulder. "I've been to Aunt Genie's and you haven't. I know exactly where to go from here. Besides, I still have the key."

"Suppose that's not Evans's bike?" Shaun asked, hurrying to catch up. "Or if it is, what if he's not at your aunt's apartment?"

"Then we won't have wasted more than a minute or two," she said, breaking into a trot. "Come on!"

Shaun let Delia lead till they were nearly to the apartment door, then he grabbed her firmly and shoved her behind him. The look on her face was part consternation, part resentment. He didn't let that stop him. Though he wasn't an expert in motorcycles, he had great distance vision and a good memory for numbers. The tiny license plate on the black bike identified it as belonging to the man they were after. There was no question.

When Delia started to protest, Shaun laid his index finger against his lips and hissed, "Shush."

Making a face, she nonetheless obeyed. Shaun didn't know how long her voluntary compliance would continue but at least she was letting him take the lead for the moment. That was definitely a plus.

He bent closer to whisper, "I'll go in first. You hang back." The defiance in her gaze made him add, "Please?" and hesitate until she nodded and handed him the key.

Peering past him, she gave a disgusted-sounding, "Humph."

Shaun followed her line of sight and noticed that the apartment door was ajar. From the looks of the splintered jamb, the building maintenance crew was going to be in need of a good carpenter.

He spread his arms, using his left to ease open the door and his right to block Delia's access to the opening.

In the dimly lit interior he was able to discern only one man; the one they had anticipated.

Shaun was relieved. He'd bested small groups of adversaries in the past but he wasn't looking forward to that much of a challenge this time. Not when he also had a headstrong woman to protect. If he didn't put Evans out of commission with a couple of well-placed blows, as he had in Maine, there was every chance Delia would dive into the melee and get herself hurt trying to help.

Evans had his back to the door and was busy stuffing small items into a gym bag. Shaun assumed he intended to steal whatever he could carry on the motorcycle, then perhaps come back for the larger stuff, like the DVD player, TV and computer, when he had a better way to haul it.

He eased into the room, careful to make no noise. Though he sensed Delia behind him, he didn't dare take his eyes off Evans for an instant. Advantages in situations like this were measured in microseconds.

The apartment was strewn with the remnants of what had once been expensive furniture. The cream-colored leather couch had been slashed, the occasional chairs reduced to kindling. In the middle of the room, blocking direct access to his quarry, a glass-topped, wrought iron coffee table had been upended and smashed in an apparent fit of temper.

If Evans was responsible for the damage, Shaun sincerely hoped the thorough ransacking had used up a lot of the other man's energy. This was one fight the good guys couldn't afford to lose.

He sidestepped the glass shards and closed the distance soundlessly. Twenty feet—eighteen—fifteen. Shaun held his breath. He was almost close enough to use a chokehold and render his opponent unconscious without taking him on hand to hand.

Something made a tinkling, shuffling sound behind him. Shaun glanced back for a split second. Delia had apparently nudged a bit of broken glass with the toe of her sneaker because she was giving him an apologetic look. Suddenly, her eyes widened in alarm.

Shaun whirled in time to see Erik Evans braced for battle. The man's chunky body hit him squarely in the chest and they both went down with mingled shouts and a resounding thud.

Evans landed atop Shaun, knocking the air out of him. Before Shaun could react, the other man had grabbed his hair and was smashing the back of his head against the floor.

Shaun saw a leg from one of the splintered chairs arc through the air above his opponent's back and heard it connect with a dull *whop* before glancing off his shoulder.

Delia! Now she'd done it. Evans was sure to turn on her!

Shaun filled his lungs as soon as the thug pushed himself off his chest and used the first breath to shout, "Run! Get out of here!"

Naturally, she ignored him. He struggled to his feet in time to see her bouncing across the seat of the slashed couch like a barefoot Polynesian native crossing hot coals. She had the chair leg raised as if she were about to bat a home run.

When Evans lunged toward Delia, Shaun tackled the heavyset man at the knees and brought him down. Hard. The *whish* of the chair leg whirring past Shaun's ear did not inspire confidence in Delia's aim.

"Hey! Watch what you're doing!"

"I am. Move so I can hit him again," she demanded.

Shaun twisted Evans's left arm behind him, put his knee in the small of the man's back and used the leverage to pin him to the floor, facedown. "You don't need to. I've got him." Now that he had regained the upper hand he found the situation amusing. "You're a bloodthirsty little thing, aren't you?"

"I was saving you, you stubborn—"

"I'd have been fine if you hadn't tipped him off that we were sneaking up on him."

"I tripped."

"I gathered."

He stood, hoisting Evans to his feet while keeping tension on his disjointed arm.

The criminal wailed. "Ow! Take it easy. You don't need to break it, man."

"Maybe I will anyway, just for practice," Shaun threatened. "Or maybe I'll hold you still and let my friend, here, get even. If I remember right, she can hit a baseball right out of the park when she connects."

"She'll kill me!"

"Not if you cooperate. Right Delia?"

To Shaun's delight, she was playing along as well as if they'd rehearsed it. Stance wide, she was holding the chair leg like a bat and rhythmically smacking its wider end onto her opposite palm.

"Maybe. Maybe not. I'd like to hear what he has to say before I make any promises."

"Okay, okay. Just call her off, man. I'll tell you whatever you want to know. I got nothin' to hide."

"Then why did you run?" Delia asked. "Why didn't you keep your promise and meet with my father?"

He regarded her as if he thought she was dim-witted. "Look, lady, I didn't have time to hang around in Maine. I had to make it back here before somebody else cleaned out all the expensive stuff and left me with junk."

"That's not good enough," Delia said. "My father's lawyers got you out of jail because you said you had inside information about Genie. You owe it to me."

"You ain't gonna tell the cops?"

Instead of answering, she raised the bat.

"Okay, okay," Evans said. "It's your word against mine, anyway. Genie was a gambling buddy of mine from way back. She looked me up one day and said she needed help to get control of her crazy sister, Trudy. That's all it was. I promise."

The mention of her mother's name made Delia freeze.

Shaun spun the man around, pushed him onto the sofa, then stood over him. "What about Trudy?"

"That was the job I did, man. The one I never got paid for." Evans was rubbing his sore wrist as he spoke. "Genie told me her sister was nuts and she needed help getting her back from California. So I went to Santa Barbara and sort of persuaded Trudy to come with me."

Shaun glared at him. "She trusted you enough to let you haul her off, is that what you're saying?"

"Hey, I didn't hurt her. And I didn't take her far," Evans insisted. "I turned her over to Genie real quick."

"Then what happened?"

"I don't know. The last I saw them, Genie had drugged her sister, loaded her into her car and was headed east. We were supposed to meet back here in a week so she could pay me. Only she never showed." He cringed under Shaun's intense stare. "That's the truth, man, I swear it."

Shaun looked to Delia. "What do you think?"

"I don't know," she said with a sigh. "Now that Genie's dead we may never find out what she did with my mother."

"I'd try that hospital where she used to be locked

up," Evans volunteered. "The one in Chicago. I think Genie said she was planning to take her back there. It figures. It was on the way."

"That still doesn't explain how Genie eventually ended up in Maine. Dead."

"Hey, I've told you everything I know," Evans insisted. "I got no reason to lie. There's nothin' in it for me. Not anymore."

"Nothing except a possible prison term for kidnapping," Shaun said. He held out his hand and Delia took it. Together they began to edge away.

"You can't prove a thing," Evans said.

"Which is why we're going to let you go." Shaun felt Delia's fingers tighten and gave her hand an encouraging squeeze. "When we get outside, we're going to count to ten and then phone the police. I suggest you gather up your loot and hit the road."

"Okay, okay."

"And you'd better have told us the truth," Shaun warned. "The Blanchards can afford the best detectives in the world. If we want you, we can find you no matter where you try to hide. Got that?"

"Yeah, I got it." He rose stiffly and shook slivers of glass off his jeans. "Try to do a simple favor for a friend and look what happens. It ain't right."

"It could be worse," Shaun reminded him. "You could be pushing up daisies in a cemetery like your buddy, Genie."

Delia didn't realize how exhausted she was till she'd sat in the SUV for a few minutes and calmed down. They had notified the police about the break-in, as Shaun had promised, but hadn't waited around for their arrival.

He pulled to a stop at a traffic signal and asked her, "Okay. Now what? It's your call."

"Chicago," she said without hesitation. "I have to know if my mother's there. Bianca didn't have much luck when she and Leo visited Westside Medical Retreat but a lot has happened since then." She smiled wistfully. "And I have you with me for backup. We can always sit on the doctor or hit him with a chair leg if he won't tell us anything."

Shaun returned her grin. "You really are something in a fight, Delia."

"Except for the fact I almost clobbered you, you mean?"

He rubbed his ear as if it hurt. "Yeah. That was too close for comfort. I'm glad you were on my side."

Her smile gentle, she laid her hand over his where it gripped the steering wheel. "I can't tell you how glad I am that you agreed to come with me, Shaun. You didn't have to do it." She hesitated, then asked, "Why did you?"

"Beats me. I guess your father caught me in a weak moment. After he apologized for being such a…never mind. Anyway, after he apologized, I was so off balance I didn't think to refuse outright. Then, when you phoned and I realized you thought I'd agreed, I had to go ahead with it."

Delia nodded sadly. As she had suspected, Shaun

had felt obligated to accompany her. It wasn't a new phenomenon in her life. People always bowed to the wishes of Ronald Blanchard. Whether they consciously considered his wealth or not, they never overlooked his power. Everybody knew her family could buy and sell Stoneley ten times over, if they wanted to, which meant they could also ruin anyone who crossed them. Few put that power to the test.

It had been nice to dream that Shaun had come with her because he cared for her as strongly as she did for him. Reality wasn't nearly as romantic, but it was far more sensible. The best thing she could do was focus on that instead of letting her imagination make more out of Shaun's involvement than it should.

Delia shivered. Watching him being knocked down by that low-life thug had nearly burst her heart. If she'd had any doubt that she still cared about Shaun, it had been banished in that pivotal moment. She hadn't given her own safety a second's thought. All her senses had been bent on making sure of Shaun's wellbeing.

You'd have defended anyone in that position, she argued. Yes, she would have. Her sense of right and wrong wasn't in question. The problem was her motives. She'd come to Shaun's aid because he mattered to her, not because he was simply someone in need of assistance. That was the crux of the issue.

And that was what she knew was going to keep her up many a night, even after all this was over and they'd each returned to the lives they'd been leading before this ill-advised quest had begun.

* * *

According to the directional system in the SUV, they were still a long day's drive from Chicago and it was getting dark.

Delia wasn't thrilled about spending much more time alone in the car with Shaun. She also wasn't happy about the prospect of checking into a hotel with him, separate rooms notwithstanding. It would have been nice if she could have come up with a sensible alternative. Unfortunately, their current circumstances gave her little or no wiggle room.

"If we'd been in Maine when we got Evans to talk, we could have flown from Bangor to O'Hare much faster," she remarked as he drove west. "I think that's what Bianca and Leo did."

"Like I said before, by the time we went back there and caught a plane we'd have lost another day at least, depending on available flights. Traveling this way has to be as fast, probably faster."

She had to admit Shaun was right. "I know. And I wouldn't have wanted to leave Father's car parked at an airport in New York and fly from there, either. It just seems like this drive is taking forever."

"Yeah, tell me about it."

"I thought I just did."

"Was that what that was? I thought you were just making noise because you can't stand silence."

"I'm not the one babbling right now."

"That's because you know I'm right."

"Ha! That'll be the day."

"What will?"

"The day I admit you're right," Delia said.

"Very funny."

"I thought so." She gave him a half smile as a reward for his clever banter. "You know, I always did enjoy the games you and I used to play, Shaun. That's one of the things I've missed the most."

His head snapped around. "I beg your pardon?"

Blinking, she realized belatedly that he had taken her innocent comment the wrong way. "Word games, Murphy. Word games. What did you think I meant?"

"Never mind."

The intensity of his gaze warmed her face like the Hawaiian sun. She laughed nervously. "Maybe we should talk about this."

"About what?"

"Us. You and me?"

"What's to talk about?"

"My point, exactly," Delia said. "I know we've kind of fallen back into our comfort zone with each other, but we need to remember that we're not the same people we used to be. We're not young, we're not foolish and we're *definitely* not married."

He huffed. "I'll agree to two out of three. We're not young and we're not married. As for being foolish, I don't know about you, but I'm feeling pretty dumb for agreeing to come with you."

"I'm sorry," she said quietly. "I know you felt pressured to do it and you don't want to be here, but..."

"Whoa. Hold on." Shaun eyed her surreptitiously. "Where'd you get that idea? I never said that."

"Yes, you did."

"When?"

Delia spread her hands wide in front of her, palms up. "I don't remember exactly. After we left Genie's you said something about being too shocked to turn down my father's offer of this so-called job."

"That didn't mean I wouldn't have come with you if you'd been the one to ask."

"It didn't?"

"Of course not."

"Oh." Her mind was spinning while her heart thumped so loudly she was certain Shaun must be able to hear it over the engine noise. "Well, in that case, thanks again."

"You're welcome. Again." He smiled over at her. "What's plan B? Are we going to alternate driving and sleeping and keep going like we have been? Or are you going to use Daddy's credit card and buy us a couple of swank rooms?"

"I'd love to keep driving," Delia said," but I know how tired I am and you must be running out of energy, too. I think the safest thing to do is to stop and rest."

"You're the boss, as I believe I've said before."

"You said it but you didn't mean it."

"How do you know that?"

"Because, when we caught Evans ransacking my aunt's apartment you pushed me behind you and insisted on taking charge." She could tell by the consternation in his expression that she was right. "Well? Didn't you?"

Shaun shrugged. "Okay. So maybe I was a little heavy-handed."

"A little? You ordered me to stay in the car!"

"And you did exactly the opposite."

"Of course I did. You should know by now that I have a mind of my own."

"Then use it," he countered, sobering. "The next time there's a clear danger, step back and let me handle things."

"Is that an order?"

He shook his head. "No. It's a suggestion from somebody who doesn't want to see you get hurt."

"In that case," Delia said, secretly touched, "I'll consider it."

SEVEN

Shaun wondered if he'd been too blunt. Probably. That kind of honesty was a failing of his. Then again, he could have done worse. He could have told her how beautiful he thought she was, or how impressed he'd been by her bravery while under attack. Or he could have tried to explain how deeply he wished they had managed to thwart her father and stay married. Of all the things he'd refrained from saying, that was the hardest one to accept.

He knew Delia didn't really want to revisit their failed marriage, however brief it had been. If she'd wanted to, she'd certainly have explored the subject in depth before this. The woman loved to talk. And he loved to hear her voice, to share the wordplay she was so good at. Being with her was actually fun. She made him smile whenever he managed to tear his mind away from their unhappy past. And she was resilient. In spite of everything she'd already been through she could still make jokes to lift both their moods. Delia Blanchard was an extraordinary woman. He just wished he was still calling her Delia *Murphy*.

And speaking of last names…Delia had chosen a hotel where the valet parking attendants dressed better than he did. When she had registered in the sumptuous, Persian-carpeted lobby and paid with her father's credit card, the desk clerk behind the polished marble counter had assumed too much and had politely addressed Shaun as Mr. Blanchard!

It didn't help that Delia had found the whole exchange terribly amusing.

They had little luggage so Shaun had carried his small duffel and her overnight bag up to their rooms rather than let one of the bellmen handle them.

He paused in the hallway in front of a set of side-by-side doors while she tested the keycard. He could hear her laughing softly.

"Well, this one works, *Mr. Blanchard,*" she taunted, turning to him with a wide grin as soon as she'd opened the door. "I almost died when he called you that. Your face turned so red I was afraid you were about to blow your stack."

"You didn't correct him."

"I figured it was best to leave well enough alone and not complicate matters, especially since we were using someone else's credit card."

"When you're right, you're right." Shaun followed her into the hotel room and put her over-night bag on the settee. The place was so perfectly decorated, so lavishly furnished, it reminded him of her family's estate in Stoneley. No wonder she'd chosen to stop at an establishment like this. And no wonder he felt so decidedly out of place.

"You take this room," Shaun said. "I'll bunk next door."

"They're supposed to be exactly the same so it really doesn't matter," Delia said, handing him one of the keycards. "If you decide to order room service, don't pay for it, charge it to the room so I can settle up in the morning."

"Right." *So much for sharing a nice, private meal and some in-depth conversation. Oh, well.* He edged toward the door. "Good night, then."

"Good night, Shaun."

To his chagrin, she had held back and let him shut the door himself rather than come closer. It couldn't be because she was afraid of him, he reasoned. If anything, she was too casual, too familiar. As she'd mentioned earlier, they had fallen back into some of their old habits of comfortable camaraderie.

Yeah, like the time he had taken her hand to lead her away from her aunt's condo and she'd let him. Or the times when she'd stepped into his arms as if it were the most natural thing in the world. Shaun's breathing grew ragged. He had to stop thinking about Delia and himself as a couple or the tension of being together was going to kill him.

Stepping up to his hotel room door, he slid the keycard into the slot and waited for the green light to signal that it had worked. Nothing happened. He withdrew the card and tried again, this time removing it as he'd seen Delia do.

Still nothing. He tried and failed repeatedly, then snorted in self-derision. Terrific. Here he was, in a place that was so fancy-schmancy it made his skin crawl, and it looked as though he was going to have to ask for help getting his stupid room unlocked. Well, *Mr. Blanchard* was not going back down to the lobby to see if they'd given him a bad card until he'd exhausted all other options. He'd rather look foolish to Delia than to the stuffed shirt who had checked them in.

Stifling his pride, Shaun knocked on her door. "Delia? It's me."

She opened the door against its protective chain and peered out. "Shaun? What's wrong?"

"My key won't work."

"It should have. I…" She eased the door closed enough to release the chain, then swung it wide. "Oops. I think I gave you the one I used."

"You gave me the key to *your* room?"

"Not on purpose," she insisted. "Hold on a sec. I'll check."

When she turned to face him and held up another card, still in its envelope, Shaun was delighted to see the rosy blush warming her cheeks. He stepped closer than he needed to and accepted it. "You gave me the key to your room."

"I told you. It was an accident."

"Freud would have a field day with that kind of accident," he said softly.

"Well, the man is long dead so I don't think he'll have much to say about it."

"Maybe not, but I do."

"Shaun…don't look at me like that."

"Like what? I just came to get the right key."

"Then why are you still standing there?"

"Because I want to kiss you. I've wanted to kiss you ever since that morning you ran off the road and landed in the bushes."

"You have?"

Shaun heard surprise in her tone but not rejection. "Yes. I have."

"It's probably not a good idea," Delia said, sounding a bit breathless.

"It's probably a terrible idea." To his delight, she hadn't retreated. He set his duffel bag on the floor at his side and opened his arms.

"I wish you hadn't asked me," Delia whispered, coming closer.

"Why not?"

"Because, this way, I have to actually decide instead of just…"

"Stop talking and come here," Shaun said tenderly.

One more step and she was in his arms. Enfolding her in a light embrace, he felt as unsure and shaky as a teenager on a blind date. Delia wasn't the first woman he'd ever kissed, nor had she been the last. She was simply the most important. She always had been.

Delia knew she was crazy to respond to Shaun's request for a kiss but she was so tired of fighting her feelings for him. Truth be told, she wanted that kiss more than anything.

Logic kept insisting that it probably wasn't going to be nearly as wonderful as she had imagined. Why, it might even help her get him out of her system once and for all. Memories of lost loves were always better than reality had been and she was certain that she had remembered Shaun's kisses as much more breathtaking than they really were.

She closed her eyes and tilted her face up to him. His breath was warm and sweet on her skin. Her lashes fluttered. Her heart sped. What was taking him so long? In the past, he'd always been quick to act. Now, he seemed to be operating in slow motion.

Delia's hands had been pressed flat to his chest. She pushed them up and threaded her fingers into Shaun's thick hair, relishing the opportunity to touch the man who had, for a short, lovely time, belonged to her. And she, to him.

When she heard Shaun moan and felt him tighten his hold she realized she'd made a tactical error. He hadn't been hesitant to kiss her, he'd been struggling to control himself.

Something inside Delia flared like a campfire on a starlit beach. It was as if her whole being had been waiting twelve long years for Shaun's kiss. And what a kiss it was!

He didn't crush her lips awkwardly, the way he used to when she was seventeen. Instead, his mouth barely grazed hers, exploring, claiming, then finally settling as though it knew exactly where it belonged. A more perfect, heartwarming, inspiring kiss would have been impossible.

Delia was afraid to breathe, to move a muscle, for fear she'd destroy the tenuous mood. If she had honestly believed that this kiss would prove that her memories of Shaun had been inflated, she'd been seriously deluded.

Denying that the man was making an impression that would follow her every day of her life was futile. However, she knew she wasn't ready to take their relationship any further. Nor was she the kind of person who would lead a man on only to end up pushing him away because she knew that going too far and becoming intimate was wrong, outside of marriage.

There was only one rational way to deal with the situation. Somehow, she'd have to convince Shaun that she wasn't deeply affected by his amazing kiss. That would give them both an easy out and perhaps preserve their developing friendship. It wasn't a foolproof notion but it was the best she could come up with when her senses were on overload and her moral compass hardly knew up from down.

Pushing him away slightly, she leaned back, opened her eyes and smiled. "Whew! I see you've been practicing."

He looked flustered. "What?"

"Your kissing. I don't know who your teacher was but she gets my vote." To Delia's regret, his expression hardened and the tender eagerness went out of his eyes.

"Thanks," he said. "I'll tell her you approve."

"Is it somebody I know?" she asked, when she really wanted to say, *Whoever she is, I hate her.*

Shaun shrugged noncommittally. "I've traveled the world in the past twelve years, Delia. I guess I've picked up a few things along the way."

"I guess you have. Well, see you in the morning." The way he was hesitating made Delia wonder if he was going to argue or try to kiss her again. To her disappointment, he did neither.

Instead, he held out his hand. "Here's your key. If you'll wait just a second while I go try the other one, I won't bother you anymore."

"Hey, no bother," she said lightly, hoping she could hold back the telltale moisture pooling behind her lashes until she was alone.

She watched him pick up his duffel and followed him to the door. "I'll stand right here and watch till you're in."

Shaun jammed the keycard into the lock on his door, jerked it open and disappeared inside without another word.

Backing into her own room, Delia closed the door and leaned against it. She couldn't decide who she was more furious with—herself, or the maddening man who had just kissed his way back into her already turbulent life. Was it possible that they were being given a second chance at love after all this time?

She swiped at a stray tear. A second chance? Them? Who was she kidding? She and Shaun had no prospects of happiness together. He was an avowed drifter who was only accompanying her because he was protecting his father's business interests, no matter what he claimed. If he did stay in

Stoneley to help Ian it wouldn't matter because she lived half a world away.

Besides, she reasoned, pausing to blow her nose and hoping Shaun couldn't hear her through their common wall, she'd promised herself she'd never get involved with a man whose beliefs didn't echo hers. To listen to Shaun lately, a person would think he didn't believe in God at all, let alone still practice the faith they had once shared.

"We're totally wrong for each other. So why am I crying?

"Because I love him anyway," she answered with disgust. "I don't want to, I didn't mean to, and I know it's crazy, but I love him."

Still sniffling, she rummaged through her overnight bag till she found her stash of candy bars. Tomorrow, she'd have to stop and stock up on more chocolate. The little she'd brought with her was going to be both her dinner and her solace. If she couldn't have real love, she'd settle for the chemicals in the candy that mimicked it.

"*That's* what they should have eaten in the Garden of Eden," she said, a little surprised at the convoluted turn of thought. "An apple is not nearly the temptation that a chocolate bar is."

And no candy can compare to the temptation brooding in the next room, she added silently.

Like it or not, the rest of her trip with Shaun was going to be a lot more difficult than it had been so far. The kindest thing she could do, for both their sakes, was to keep her distance. She just wasn't sure she could continue the pretense of not caring about him without coming seriously unglued.

The best thing that she could do, in her opinion, was to keep an emotional distance between them. Shaun had left her in a huff. If she was lucky, he'd stay angry and she'd be able to muster enough gruffness to mirror his mood and carry them both through the coming days.

She peeled back the wrapper on the first candy bar and plunked down on the edge of her king-size bed to drown her sorrows in chocolates. Good thing she was active and had a rapid metabolism so she could get away with eating like this once in a while and not get too *momona,* too *fat.* Nobody'd trust a chubby surfing instructor.

"No, but I'd probably float better," she said cynically. "Yeah, and look like a beached whale in my bathing suit!"

That was not the professional image she sought to project but right now she figured she needed the chocolate's uplift more than she needed to avoid a few more ounces. Never mind that the Bible listed the drunkard and the glutton as equal sinners in Proverbs! She had to eat something and the candy was handy.

Two and a half candy bars later, Delia heard a knock. She ignored it until it was repeated. Padding to the door on bare feet she peered out the peephole. Her jaw dropped.

"Room service," Shaun said.

"I didn't order any food."

"I figured you wouldn't. You never did eat right when you were upset."

"I'm not hungry."

"You have to keep your strength up."

"I ate."

"What?"

"Candy."

"That's not food," Shaun insisted. "Come on. Open the door. This pizza's getting cold."

"You eat it."

"I fully intend to. With you. Now, are you going to open the door or do I have to make a scene out here?"

"You wouldn't."

"Oh, really?"

She strained to see his face through the tiny peephole. She knew that look. He wasn't exactly grinning but he wasn't grumpy anymore, either. And he was definitely determined to get her to eat, one way or another.

Resigned to her fate, Delia unhooked the safety chain and opened the door. Before she could argue further, Shaun sidled past her, crossed the room and placed a pizza box on the round table by the window.

"I got a special deluxe because that was what they had already cooked in the quick-stop next door," he said. "If you don't like any of the toppings, just scrape them off. I won't mind."

She hung back by the open door. "I told you. I'm full."

"Yeah, I see." He fisted the candy wrappers and dropped them into the wastebasket. "What kind of diet is that?"

"Chocolate lover's," Delia shot back, not caring that she sounded defensive.

"Well, I'm going to eat, even if you're not." He pulled two bottles of cold soda from his jacket pockets and set them on the table next to the pizza.

A perverse side of Delia's personality kept insisting she wasn't going to let Shaun coerce her into eating with him. A more rational side reminded her that he was trying to be nice, possibly to make amends for kissing her.

The thought of his kiss rose like a wisp of smoke and coiled in her already crowded stomach, making her wish mightily that she'd stopped after the first candy bar.

Truthfully, she did crave something that wasn't sweet tasting. And the pizza smelled wonderful.

"Okay," she said, approaching the table. "But we're leaving the door open."

"Fine with me. I just came here to eat."

"You didn't want to use room service?"

"Nope. This meal is on me. My treat." He smiled as he lifted a triangular slice and used his other hand to loop hanging strings of cheese over it before taking a bite. "Guess my bourgeois roots are showing, huh?"

Delia couldn't help returning his smile. "Nothing wrong with a few simple pleasures, Murphy. I'm sure you remember how much I love pizza."

"I remember." He looked away. "I would have bought one with pineapple on it, in honor of your adopted state, if they'd had that available."

"Actually, there are very few pineapple plantations in Hawaii anymore. No sugarcane, either. All that kind of farming has moved to places like the Philippines."

"Really? Well, there goes the neighborhood, as they say. What do the Islands rely on now, just tourism?"

"For the most part. We have some cattle ranches and truck farms, of course, but the big plantations are history." She took a chair across from him, lifted a slice of the delectable treat and bit into it before she said, "At home, I often order pizza with shrimp on it."

The odd expression on Shaun's face made her laugh. "It's an acquired taste. We eat a lot of seafood in the Islands. There aren't any native lobsters, like there are in Maine, but we have our share of delicacies."

"Besides candy bars?" He arched an eyebrow and glanced at the wastebasket. "I can't believe you ate all that junk."

"Neither can I," Delia admitted ruefully. "I hate to say this, but I'm glad you brought me some real food."

"It's not caviar," he said quietly.

"No," Delia replied. "It's the kind of food old friends can share without worrying about getting their fingers messy or being too formal. This reminds me of some of the great times you and I used to have a long time ago."

"Good," Shaun said, averting his gaze while he continued to eat ravenously. "It was supposed to."

EIGHT

Delia had slept poorly after their impromptu pizza party. She wasn't sure whether her insomnia had been because of all she'd eaten or because of who she'd eaten it with. Whatever the cause, she'd been struggling to stay awake from the moment they'd piled back into the SUV to continue their trip the following morning.

She'd been letting the motion of the car lull her to sleep while Shaun drove in silence. The cessation of motion roused her when he finally pulled up to the iron gates of Westside Medical Retreat and stopped. "Are we there?"

"Looks like it."

"Umm." Stretching, she blinked rapidly to focus. Her mouth was dry and her head ached. "Okay," she said, reaching for a bottle of water to quench her thirst while she braced herself for what was to come. "Let's go on in."

"You're sure you're ready?"

"No, but I'm going through with this anyway."

Nodding as if in agreement, he drove past the open gates and followed the winding, tree-lined drive that led to the Tudor-style, brick-and-stone hospital.

Delia's heart sank the moment they rounded the final corner and she got a good look at the place. It may once have been majestic but it had deteriorated until it was run-down and seedy-looking, just as her sister Bianca had described.

Moss splotched the reddish brick walls, making them appear darker and horribly dingy. The banks of small windows facing the front were multipaned, reminding her of the many-faceted eyes of a predatory insect.

She glanced at Shaun. "This whole place gives me the creeps."

"Yeah. I know what you mean. Hopefully, the inside is better than the outside."

"I wouldn't count on it."

Shaun brought the SUV to a stop parallel to the dull, beige stone portico denoting the front entrance. Delia shed her seat belt and gripped the door handle.

Shaun made no move to do likewise so she asked, "Aren't you coming?"

"Do you want me to?"

"Of course."

"Then I will."

She had to bite her lip to keep from snapping at him. Between her uneasiness over the present situation and her memories of their conflict and eventual truce the previous evening, she was an emotional wreck.

Still, the last thing she wanted to do was waltz into the mental institution alone to face whatever awaited her. Not only did she crave moral support, she wanted Shaun to provide it. No one else would do. If she'd had a troop of armed superheroes surrounding her, she'd still have wanted Shaun at her side. It was just a bit galling to have to *ask* him to accompany her.

Delia slung the strap of her purse over her right shoulder and waited for him to circle the SUV before she started toward the massive double doors.

There were no welcome signs posted, no instructions for visitors, nothing but a brass nameplate, Westside Medical Retreat, and an ornate bell with a chain hanging beside the doors.

She sensed, rather than felt, Shaun's hand at the small of her back and looked to him. "Should we ring?"

He reached to open the door and found it locked. "I was going to say, no, but we seem to have no choice."

Delia rang the bell. Repeatedly. Finally, a gray-haired woman in a nurse's uniform opened the door slightly and peered out.

"Saturday is visiting day," the woman said. "Deliveries go around the back."

Taking both Delia and the nurse by surprise, Shaun gave the door a hard push and barged in. "Today just became visiting day. We want to see the doctor in charge. Now."

"I'm sorry, sir, that will be impossible. Dr. Brooks is a very busy man. You'll need an appointment."

"Consider this our appointment." Shaun's voice was throaty and tinged with antagonism. If Delia had been in the nurse's place and hadn't known what a sweet guy he was, his demeanor would have frightened her enough to convince her he was deadly serious—and probably dangerous.

"Wait here. I'll see what I can do. Perhaps our administrator, Mrs. Greeley, is free to speak with you."

"Why don't we just tag along while you find out and save you the trip back to get us?" Shaun's polite smile didn't reach the steely blue of his eyes.

"I could call security."

Delia didn't want Shaun to wind up in jail—or hurt—so she intervened. "Please, don't feel you have to do that. We don't want any trouble. We're simply concerned about one of your former patients. We promise we won't take up much of the doctor's time."

"Very well. This way."

Shaun took Delia's arm and they fell in behind the nurse. He leaned closer to whisper, "Good cop, bad cop?"

"No," she told him aside. "Finesse."

"Ah. I see. Did they teach you that in finishing school?"

"No. I learned how to be polite at home."

"And I didn't? Is that what you're saying?"

Delia made a face at him. "Knock it off, Murphy. Everybody knows you can catch more flies with honey than you can with vinegar. You don't have to go to a fancy school to learn that."

"Point taken."

The hallway was long, bare and dimly lit. The walls were a color that was probably supposed to be a muted green but had turned out to be more of a sickly gray, and the floor was a shiny checkerboard of brown and beige vinyl. Each door they passed had a small window of reinforced glass at eye level but none of the rooms stood open. Delia suspected that the doors were locked to keep the patients inside. The thought of being confined to one sparsely furnished room and unable to leave it at will gave her the shivers and made her stomach queasy.

The next time she stood on a wide expanse of beach and felt the freedom of the wind in her hair, the warm sun on her face, she was going to raise her hands to heaven and thank God. Literally.

The nurse paused at a door with Administration stenciled in gold lettering on a smoky glass panel. She knocked cautiously. When a female voice from inside called, "Come in," the nurse entered partway and paused, blocking Delia and Shaun's access with her body.

"There are some visitors here," she said. "They insist on seeing Dr. Brooks."

"Show them in. I'll take care of it."

The nurse stepped aside. "Mrs. Greeley will see you."

Delia could tell that Shaun was about to reiterate his demand to meet with the doctor so she quickly took charge and offered her hand to the prim, older woman behind the desk. "Mrs. Greeley. Thank you for agreeing to speak with us on such short notice. We've come a long way and this is a matter of utmost importance."

"And you are?" the other woman asked without accepting Delia's offer to shake hands.

"Delia Blanchard. I believe you met my older sister, Bianca, a few months ago."

"I have no recollection of doing so. What is your business here?"

"It's about my mother. Trudy—Gertrude—Blanchard? She was a patient of yours for many years."

"I'm afraid I can neither confirm nor deny that, Ms. Blanchard. We never give out patient information."

"My sister spoke privately with a Dr. Brooks. We wish to do the same," Delia said firmly. She clasped her trembling fingers together to still them and present an image of calm assurance. No one must suspect she was putting on an act, least of all the hospital personnel.

Shaun, however, had apparently sensed her uneasiness because he stepped up beside her to offer silent support.

"Dr. Brooks is a busy man," the administrator said.

"So we've been told," Delia replied. "Perhaps he will agree to see us if you mention my aunt, Genie Hall."

Delia had thrown out the name as a test, just to see what might happen. She had expected a mild reaction at best, so she was astounded when the woman jumped to her feet and hurried toward a side door.

"Wait here," was all Mrs. Greeley said as she left the office.

Shaun leaned closer to Delia. "Whoa. You really lit a fire under her."

"Yes. She may not remember meeting Bianca but good old Aunt Genie sure got her attention."

"That's a positive sign."

"I hope so. It could also mean that Genie has been here and caused trouble of some sort."

"It couldn't be any worse than the trouble she caused in your father's library."

"That's true."

The door through which Mrs. Greeley had disappeared reopened and a tall, distinguished-looking man wearing a white lab coat and dark slacks entered. He scowled at them through black-rimmed glasses.

"Ms. Blanchard? I'm Dr. Brooks. Do you know something about Genie Hall?"

"Yes. She was my aunt," Delia said, watching the doctor's reaction and noting that he suddenly seemed less confrontational and more disconcerted.

Brooks stared. "*Was?* Has something happened to her?"

"Aunt Genie passed away about a month ago."

"What?" He quickly approached the desk and leaned on it, palms down, as if he needed the support.

"You knew her." It wasn't a question. A possible

scenario had been forming in Delia's vivid imagination and she'd decided to follow up on her hunch.

"Yes, I…"

"Of course. I am sorry. I realize now that I
shouldn't have broken the news so bluntly. She
spoke of you often."

There were unshed tears in the doctor's eyes
when he looked up. "Genie told you about me?"

"Not in so many words," Delia said. "But you
were mentioned on nearly every page of her diary.
A lot of what she wrote was rather incriminating if
you catch my drift." She patted her shoulder bag as
if she had the revealing journal with her. "Aunt Genie
was quite a character. If she actually did half the
things she claimed, she should have spent most of
her life in prison."

That was enough to push the guilt-ridden man
over the edge. He removed his glasses, pinched the
bridge of his nose with his thumb and forefinger and
began to weep openly. "I—I loved her. Anything I
did was because I loved her. You have to understand
that. She had a hypnotic beauty that I just couldn't
ignore."

"I'm sure you realize that you could be arrested,"
Delia ventured, eyeing Shaun to ask for his backing.
To her relief, he understood.

"Yes," Shaun added, "and we're ready to go to the
police with what we know, unless you cooperate."

"It—it doesn't matter anymore," Brooks stut-
tered. "Nothing does. Not without my beautiful
Genie."

"You may feel that way right now," Shaun said, "but you've got a cozy little operation here. Once you've calmed down and thought about it, I imagine you'll change your tune."

He approached the doctor, grabbed him by the lapels of his lab coat and lifted him till they were nose to nose. "Tell you what, Doc. We'll make you a deal. Show us Trudy Blanchard's records and we'll give you whatever information Genie left behind to do with as you please."

Nice one, Shaun, Delia thought. *Not a lie, yet not of much use in the long run, either, since we don't have anything in writing.* She slipped her hand inside her purse and pretended to pat the nonexistent diary again. "That's right. All we want is to see the records."

"All right." Brooks relented. "Let me go. I'll show you."

Shaun eased his grip while giving the other man his most threatening stare. "No tricks."

"No tricks. I'll have the records brought to my office." He straightened his rumpled lab coat, then pointed to the door by which he had entered. "Wait in there."

Delia remembered how her sister Bianca, and Leo Santiago had "accidentally" been locked in a padded cell when they had visited the same mental hospital.

"No, thanks, doctor," she said firmly. "I think we'll stick with you, if you don't mind."

"Hah! We'll stick with him even if he *does* mind," Shaun said derisively. "No offense, Doc, but you can't really blame us if we don't trust you out of our sight."

Brooks shrugged. "I don't really care what you do." He leaned across the desk, picked up the telephone receiver and pushed a button. "This is Dr. Brooks. I want you to bring all the records for Trudy Blanchard—" he spelled the name "—to my office. Yes. Everything."

Delia couldn't hear the other end of the conversation but she heard the doctor mutter a colorful curse under his breath before he said, "No. Tomorrow isn't good enough. I want those records *yesterday.*"

Making quick eye contact with Shaun, Delia was relieved to see that she wasn't the only one exhibiting relief. The sooner they got what they'd come for and headed back to Maine, the happier they'd both be.

Ah, but I'll be happier because I'll know more about my mother, she thought. *Shaun will be happier because he'll be rid of me.*

If she could have convinced herself otherwise, she'd gladly have done so. As it was, she was stuck with a reality as stark and forbidding as the atmosphere inside the gray-green walls of the mental institution.

To Delia's consternation, her mother's hospitalization records were so copious they filled a stack of manila folders that stood over a foot high.

"Wow. It looks like this may take a while," she said, pulling a chair up to the side of the doctor's desk and plunking down in it. The paper smelled musty, as if it had absorbed the oppressive, moldy aura of the entire facility.

"Yeah." Shaun joined her while keeping an eye on Brooks. "Sit, Doc. You're staying, too."

"I have work to do, rounds to make," Dr. Brooks said.

"Then you'll make them after we're through." Shaun continued to stand until the doctor finally sat down behind his desk.

"There's no reason for me to be here," Brooks argued. "If you have any questions I can answer them later."

"Like you answered my sister Bianca's questions?" Delia replied. "No way. Shaun's right. You need to stay right here with us. I'm not going to let down my guard and wind up stuck here like my mother did."

"Your mother was ill when she first came to us," Brooks insisted.

"I see that. 'Diagnosis, postpartum depression,'" Delia read. "You must be a really lousy doctor if that lasted over twenty years."

Delia saw the doctor stiffen. He began to scowl at her. "I thought you said you'd read Genie's diary."

"Enough of it," Delia said quickly. She divided the stack of file folders and handed half to Shaun. "Here. You look through these so we can get out of here faster. This place gives me the willies."

"Why don't you start with the most recent entries?" Shaun suggested, "and give me the older ones."

"Good idea." Delia quickly inverted the stack and re-sorted the folders.

She scanned the dates in the newest one. "According to this, Mother hasn't been here for four or five months. That must have been when she escaped and went to Juliet's father for help."

Shaun eyed her. "Juliet? Your baby sister? Wait a minute. Ronald isn't her father?"

"No," Delia said. "Mother was having an affair with a college professor named Arthur Sinclair before Juliet was born. That was why my father was so angry. He and Mother had a terrible fight about it when Juliet was only a few weeks old."

"You'd told me something to that effect years ago but you'd never mentioned the underlying reasons."

"Well, that was why. Mother drove off one night in the middle of a storm and we never saw her again. Father told us she'd had a fatal auto accident. It was only recently that we learned he'd gotten a divorce and lied about what had really happened to her so we'd forget her. He didn't think she'd ever have the nerve to show her face in Stoneley again, especially after he got her to sign away her parental rights."

"Wow."

Shaun continued to scan the records. "Look at this. I don't know much about medicine but it seems to me your mother was kept pretty full of drugs. It's no wonder she didn't improve."

Delia looked at the doctor. "You saw to that. You and Genie. Right?"

"You should know," Brooks said dully.

"Genie hated my mother. She couldn't even stand to see a photo of her. That was why she poked the eyes out of the snapshots in her apartment." Delia regarded him solemnly. "How could a medical professional like you fall for a woman like Genie who was so obviously mentally unbalanced?"

"Love has nothing to do with sanity," he said.

Beside her, Delia heard Shaun mutter, "That's the first intelligent thing he's said so far."

Shaun gave up before Delia did. He shut the top folder in his dwindling pile, pushed back from the desk and stretched. "All this stuff reads alike. It's just vital signs and more medication, month after month, year after year."

She sighed. "Here, too. I was hoping…"

"I know." Getting to his feet, Shaun leaned over the desk so he was eye to eye with the doctor. "This is your problem, too, Doc. What are we missing, huh? Maybe we should bring in the authorities after all and let a professional go over your records. All of them."

"My records are in order."

"Are they? What about the financial side of things?"

"There's nothing irregular there, either."

"Suppose we take a look."

"I see no reason to accommodate you further," Brooks said.

Shaun had been afraid the doctor would regain some backbone once the shock of hearing about Genie's death wore off. Apparently, he had.

"Look," Shaun said. "We've already seen patient records that were supposed to be kept confidential.

What can it hurt to humor us and get this over with?" He stood, leaned over the desk again and arched an eyebrow. "You do want to get rid of us, don't you?"

"Nothing would make me happier," Brooks said. "All right. Follow me."

Delia was hesitant to leave the stack of folders. They were the only tangible thing she had to prove her mother's continued existence. Still, she knew she couldn't take them with her. Hopefully, Trudy's time spent in a place like this was a thing of the past, and they could all start over. If they ever found her.

Brooks led the way back into Mrs. Greeley's office. She looked surprised to see him as well as decidedly unfriendly toward his companions.

"I want you to pull up the Trudy Blanchard payment records," the doctor said.

"All of them?"

"All of them, as far back as the computer goes." He glanced at Delia. "If you need more, it will necessitate a trip to the basement. When your mother first came to us we kept our files on paper. There are stacks of boxes you'd have to go through."

"Let's start here and see what you have," Delia said, putting her purse on one of the chairs beside the desk. She knew better than to trust Brooks or his staff enough to follow any of them into a dark, secluded basement, even with Shaun to protect her.

Mrs. Greeley quickly accessed the payment records. "As you can see," she said primly, "the payments were made regularly."

Delia leaned over and peered at the screen. She didn't know what she was looking for but she was out of options. If they didn't find any clues in this file, they might as well give up—and Delia was *not* the kind of person to do that.

She pointed at the screen. "What does this number mean?"

"It's the code for the account Ms. Hall set up with us. All of Mrs. Blanchard's expenses were paid out of it."

"There were no checks? No itemized bills?"

"Ms. Hall was given itemized lists of charges. She approved them when she visited her sister and then we debited the account for that amount and mailed her the receipts." The older woman sneered at Delia. "I assure you, it was quite legitimate."

"I'm sure it was. Aunt Genie was no fool. The thing I don't understand is how she could afford to keep my mother locked up here for all those years."

"Did your father pay for it?" Shaun asked.

Delia was quick to answer, "No. Father can be a hard man, especially in business, but he would never be a party to something as spiteful and cruel as this. He hadn't heard from Mother since he divorced her and legally terminated her rights to me and my sisters."

"Maybe your Aunt Genie was wealthier than you thought."

"If she was, she hid it from her own parents," Delia said. "They thought she was broke most of the time. And we know she had an addiction to gambling. Our motorcycle-riding buddy confirmed that, remember?"

"True." Shaun scowled and leaned closer to Delia so he could study the computer monitor, too. "What does this code mean," he asked, pointing. "The one in the heading."

"Just a second. I'll look it up," Mrs. Greeley said. She pushed a few buttons, then scrolled down after a split screen appeared. "Here we are. It's the firm Ms. Hall's payments were debited to. Cymbeline Corporation."

Delia's breath caught. Wide-eyed, she looked at Shaun.

He laid his arm protectively across her shoulders. "What does it mean?"

"It's another of Shakespeare's plays," Delia explained. "A more obscure one. Imogen—Genie for short—is one of the characters in *Cymbeline*."

"Why should that upset you?" Shaun asked. "Your whole family is really into Shakespeare."

"Yes, but if Aunt Genie didn't have any money and this corporation was set up just to pay for my mother's continual torture in this awful place, that name was probably chosen by someone else who was also very knowledgeable about Shakespeare."

"So?"

"So, the only ones I know who fill that requirement are the grandparents I just met, Eleanor and Stanley Hall. They run a literary press and they raised two daughters with the names of famous characters, Trudy from *Hamlet* and Genie from *Cymbeline*."

"But, you told me they were genuinely upset, that

they were looking forward to seeing your mother again after she contacted them. Why would they claim that if they'd known where she was all along? Or if they'd been the ones paying to keep her here?"

"I don't know." Delia rubbed her tired eyes. "None of this makes sense. When I told them about the DNA results, Eleanor wept like she was truly grieving." She straightened and blinked, trying to clear her head. "Maybe she was upset because Genie had died instead of my mother."

"I don't know what to say. Do you want to call them from here and ask?"

Delia shook her head. "No. If they are responsible I don't want to give them time to think of an alibi. And I want to be looking them in the eye when I tell them what we've found."

She squared her shoulders and retrieved her purse, thanked the hospital personnel, then turned to Shaun. "We're done here. Let's go home."

NINE

Shaun wanted to say or do something that would lift Delia's spirits. He didn't know her maternal grandparents personally but he couldn't imagine that any parents would lock up their own child unless she were truly in need of extended hospitalization.

It was possible that Delia's mother had been that ill, of course, although he doubted it. The suspicious reactions of the doctor and the obvious involvement of her nefarious late aunt pretty much precluded genuine mental illness on Trudy's part. The question was, how much of what they now knew was factual, and how much was the result of a criminal conspiracy?

Seated beside him in the car, Delia had been silent for the past hour. He couldn't tell if she was brooding or simply exhausted. He knew how tired he was and he hadn't had a personal stake in their foray into the world of the infamous Dr. Brooks the way she had.

He made a conscious decision, one he was pretty sure would make Delia angry. He was willing to risk her ire under the present circumstances. After all, what were friends for if not to step in and lend a hand when a person wasn't thinking clearly?

Without announcing his plans, he stayed on Highway 88 instead of skirting greater Chicago farther to the south the way they had when they'd arrived. He knew exactly where he was going because he'd stopped in Canfield several years back to work on a construction crew that was building concession stands for the zoo.

Delia needed a break. So did he. And he didn't see any reason why they should hurry back to Maine. They'd been gone this long. What would one day's respite hurt?

Puzzled, she glanced over at him. "Where are we?"

"I was scouting for a nice hotel," Shaun said honestly. "It's getting late."

"Umm, I guess it is. Okay. Your choice this time."

"How about one near a real pizza parlor instead of a quick-stop?"

To his relief, she chuckled softly. "You do have your priorities sorted out, don't you, Murphy? All right. I really don't care."

"See that high-rise over there?" He pointed. "I recognize the name. It's a well-known hotel chain so it should suit you."

"You don't know me very well, do you?" Delia commented amiably.

"Why do you say that?"

"Because, you seem to think I'm really stuck up when I'm not."

"I was only judging by the place you picked last night."

"Oh. Well, maybe I am a little spoiled. But the way I look at it, if my father is footing the bill, we should enjoy spending his money. Lots of it."

"And why is that?"

"Because he owes us," Delia said, sobering and turning to gaze out the window at the passing city scene.

She didn't have to spell it out. Shaun knew exactly what she meant and he agreed with her one hundred percent. Ronald Blanchard owed them more than any amount of money would fix. He'd robbed them of a future together.

Delia could tell that the hotel was still fancier than Shaun would have liked but she was too tired to suggest he choose another. Besides, it was located next to a restaurant complex. They could park and walk to dinner. She wasn't about to dine with him in her room again. It was too hard on her self-control. Her brain knew they were no longer man and wife but her heart kept insisting they should still be married. Therefore, rather than revisit the internal conflict that had worn her to a frazzle twenty-four hours ago, she was going to insist they eat out.

Once again, Shaun handled their bags. Delia accompanied him to the elevator and pushed the button for their floor.

"Can I have my own key this time?" he gibed as soon as the door slid closed and they were alone.

"I'll think about it." She laughed quietly. "That was pretty funny last night. You should have seen the look on your face when you showed up back at my room because your door wouldn't open."

"I wasn't laughing."

"No, but you were sure full of blarney."

"Must be the Irish in me."

"Maybe. And maybe you're just a fun guy." She led the way into the hallway as soon as the elevator stopped.

Shaun fell into step beside her. "Which reminds me," he said. "I had an idea. While we're in the area, what do you say we take a little side trip?"

"What are you talking about?"

"We're not far from Canfield and I happen to know there's a world-class zoo there. I thought, in the morning, you might like to visit it and unwind a little."

"A zoo? What in the world made you think of that?"

"Actually, I worked on a construction crew that was hired to spruce up the place a few summers ago. It was hot and humid then but May weather's still pretty mild. I think you'd enjoy seeing this zoo. It's different. Most of the animals aren't in cages or in little areas behind moats like they are in a lot of zoos. It's more like the wilds. And there's a big butterfly house where you can walk right through the middle. The butterflies are close enough to touch. Sometimes they even light on you."

Delia didn't know what to say. "I—I don't know. I really should get home to Maine."

"And do what? Confront the grandparents you

hardly know and get embroiled in another fight? I can't imagine you're too eager to do that."

"I'm not." She paused at a room with the proper number posted on the door and turned to face Shaun. "Even if the Halls did lie to me about my mother's hospitalization, I'm sure they don't know where she is now. Eleanor was too upset and confused about the whole thing, especially when she didn't see the heirloom locket among Mother's things."

"Then that just leaves your grandfather Howard's medical condition to worry about. Why don't you phone Maine before it gets any later in the day and find out how he's doing? If he's holding his own or if they say he's better, we'll know we don't have to break any speed limits getting you back there."

Delia sighed audibly. "I'm glad one of us is thinking clearly. I will call. But I won't promise that I'll agree to go to the zoo with you."

"Fair enough. All I ask is that you consider it." He stepped back, held out his hand and smiled. "My key?"

This time, she double-checked the numbers before she handed him one of the keycards.

"You do like zoos, don't you?" Shaun asked.

"I don't know if I do or not," Delia said. "I've never been to one."

"You're kidding."

"No." She shook her head. "My father wasn't the type to take family vacations or tour places like that just for enjoyment. Not with me and my sisters, anyway. I always got the idea he thought it was a frivolous waste of time." She pulled a face. "Of course, he managed enough enthusiasm for travel to take Alannah to Europe."

"I'm sorry," Shaun said.

Delia shook her head. "Hey, don't feel sorry for me, Murphy. I escaped. If it weren't for my sisters and Aunt Winnie, I'd *never* go back to Stoneley."

"Go make your call," Shaun said flatly. "And stay away from the candy bars. When you're ready, we'll find a place close by and get some decent food."

"Sounds like a plan. See you in a few minutes."

They opened their rooms at the same time and Delia saw Shaun watching till she was safely inside. She noted that he was no longer smiling. They were both tired and stressed so that wasn't too surprising. He had seemed a lot happier when he'd first suggested the trip to the zoo, though. Perhaps he was miffed because she hadn't accepted immediately.

She wasn't sure whether she was going to give in and agree to go or not. The outing might feel too much like a date and that wasn't a good idea. Not good at all.

Then again, being away from Stoneley and temporarily carefree did appeal to her. Even if she had to pretend everything was all right, it would be nice to spend a quiet, peaceful afternoon with Shaun.

She kicked off her shoes, reached into her purse for her cell phone and flopped on the bed to relax while she made her call.

Shaun watched Delia close the door to her hotel room before he stepped into his and immediately threw his duffel onto the bed with far more force than was necessary.

Escape, she had called it. Of course. That was exactly what she had been doing when she'd agreed to elope with him in the first place. If it hadn't been him it would have been some other gullible guy. Staying in Hawaii instead of returning to the Mainland after college was how she'd turned the tables on her manipulative father and completed her so-called escape.

That one word, that one slip of the tongue, defined the whole state of affairs for Shaun more clearly than if Delia had taken pages to spell it out. Now, as then, he was merely the means to an end. Well, at least this time he was aware he was being used. He wasn't a naive, lovesick kid anymore, either. He was all grown-up.

He muttered to himself as he pulled a clean shirt from his duffel and shook out the wrinkles. Yeah, he was grown-up. The trouble was, so was Delia.

He wished mightily that he hadn't asked her to go to the zoo with him. The way his luck was running, she'd probably end up saying yes.

They strolled to a nearby restaurant that advertised barbecue as its specialty. Shaun held the door for her.

"Thanks." Delia still had no idea why he seemed so moody all of a sudden. Hopefully, he'd tell her what was bothering him during dinner. Then again, he'd always been the strong, silent type, a man who kept things to himself instead of airing grievances the way she and her sisters usually did. In that respect he was a lot like her father.

Delia rolled her eyes at the unfair comparison. Shaun was *nothing* like Ronald Blanchard. Where her father was cold, Shaun showed compassion; where her father was harsh, Shawn was forgiving.

Except in regard to our marriage, she added ruefully. That was one subject she had yet to convince him to discuss. Perhaps the topic was best left alone. Right now, they seemed to be developing an easy friendship, a camaraderie she not only enjoyed, she cherished. If they ever broached the matter of their short marriage and its rapid dissolution, there was no telling how many raw emotions would be revealed. Delia wasn't sure her overburdened mind and heart could take that much strain. Not right now, anyway.

The restaurant's dining area was dimly lit and had a rustic-chic aura, complete with small buckets of peanuts on the tables and a floor purposely littered with the empty shells. Country-western music played softly in the background.

They followed the hostess to a booth in a secluded corner and Delia slid in first, hoping Shaun would choose to sit beside her. He didn't.

She looked across the table at him and smiled. When his response was expressionless rather than amiable, she asked, "What's wrong?"

"Nothing."

"Then why do you look so down in the dumps?"

"Beats me." He drew his hand over his chin. "I shaved."

"I noticed. You look very nice."

"Presentable enough to be seen with a Blanchard daughter, you mean?"

"Just nice." Delia pulled a face. "Where did you get the chip on your shoulder? I thought we were getting along pretty well, considering."

"Considering what?" He concentrated on the menu rather than making eye contact with her.

"Considering the fact that we spent the better part of the day sitting in a creepy mental hospital and poring over my mother's old records. Give me a break, Shaun. I wasn't the one who twisted your arm to get you to come. Nobody's keeping you here, either. You can grab your bag and hop the first bus to wherever you want to go, anytime."

His head snapped up and he glowered at her. "You think I'd leave you? Just like that?"

"I don't know. You're sure acting like you'd rather be somewhere else."

"Wouldn't you?"

"Yes. But that doesn't mean I'm going to let myself take it out on you." Delia paused and sighed heavily. "The past few months have been a nightmare for me, Shaun, and I'm afraid the worst isn't over."

She had to bite the inside of her lower lip to regain control of her emotions and continue. "If you still want to go to the zoo tomorrow, it's fine with me." To her surprise, he didn't seem as happy about her decision as she'd thought he'd be.

"You're sure? What did they say about Howard when you called?"

"Nothing much. The doctors are almost ready to send him home. They just need to check the last of the reports from the tests they did. Apparently, his potassium levels were through the roof when he was admitted and that chemical imbalance upset his whole system. It could have been fatal. It nearly was."

Shaun's brow knit. "That's it? That's all they found?"

"So far. Miranda says the excess potassium would have been enough to cause his symptoms but nobody's sure how he got that way. They suspect he may have been confused and overdosed himself, although I don't know how. Peg takes care of his prescriptions and she's with him all the time."

"*All* the time?"

"Well, nearly. She's been amazingly faithful, considering how difficult Grandfather can be sometimes. Of course she can't sit with him 24-7. Sometimes our maid, Sonya Garcia, takes over and sometimes Miranda or Winnie watches him for a little while if no other professional nurses are available to relieve Peg."

"What about Juliet? Isn't she living in the house, too?"

"Yes, but she doesn't dare go near Grandfather's room. Remember? He gets delusional and thinks she's Mother."

"Oh, right. I'd forgotten. Sometimes it's hard to keep all the players straight in your family."

"Want me to have a program printed for you?"

That inane suggestion brought a lopsided grin to Shaun's handsome face and thrilled Delia all the way to her toes, inspiring her to continue. "I could run it on the computer in Father's study, print it out for you and update the file daily."

"Think that would be often enough?"

"I doubt it." She plucked a peanut from the bucket between them and crushed the brittle shell with her fingers.

Shaun followed suit. "There'd have to be lots of footnotes," he said, munching on the peanuts he'd just shelled. "Otherwise, I wouldn't know which Shakespearian play everybody was from, assuming it matters."

"Cynic." Delia lobbed an unshelled nut at him.

He ducked, laughing quietly. "Well, it's true. That business about Cymbeline Corporation is so obscure I'd have missed it completely if you hadn't been there. *Romeo and Juliet* or *Hamlet* I can handle but I'd never heard of *Cymbeline*."

"It was a tragedy," Delia said as she crushed another shell. "One of those plays where everybody is out to get everybody else and people keep getting wiped out." She gave a little huff of derision. "Actually, it's a lot like what's been happening behind the scenes in my family for as long as I can remember."

Delia dawdled through dinner and toyed with the dessert she'd ordered. Anything but say good-night to Shaun and go back to the lonely solitude of her room.

He had long since finished eating and had already paid the tab so she figured she'd better declare herself full before he lost patience. She pushed away her partially eaten slice of lemon pie, wiped her mouth on the linen napkin and laid it on the table beside the plate.

"Are you done?" he asked.

"I guess so. I'm stuffed."

"Too many peanuts," Shaun said, smiling. He stood and tossed a generous tip on the table. "For a little person you sure can pack in the food."

"I'm active. At least most of the time." Delia grabbed the strap of her purse and slid out of the booth. "I think one of the reasons I've been so out of sorts is because I've been sitting around too much."

"Well, we'll fix that tomorrow. The Canfield Zoo is spread over acres and acres."

She arched an eyebrow and smiled back at him as he held the exit door for her. "Oh? Are you sure you can keep up with me?"

"If I get too tired we'll take the tram," Shaun answered. "We may want to anyway. I don't think we can see everything in one day if we don't ride through part of it."

"Okay. Then I guess we'd better get to bed. Her cheeks reddened and she suddenly felt overly warm in spite of the cool evening air. "I mean…"

He laughed heartily. "I know what you meant,

Delia. We're both beat. Even if you gave me your key tonight I'd be too tired to take advantage of you."

"I know you'd never do that anyway," she said seriously. "It's fun to tease but we both know right from wrong."

And just because something feels as if it's right doesn't make it so, she added to herself. *Like when I defied my father and ran off with you.*

Oh, God forgive me, she continued, blinking back unshed tears and hoping Shaun didn't notice, *I wish I could go back and do exactly the same thing again.*

TEN

Judging by the approach to the Canfield Zoo, Delia wasn't all that impressed. By the time she and Shaun were inside, however, she'd changed her mind.

They'd emerged from a tunnel-like entrance into a veritable Garden of Eden. Some of the plants even reminded her of those indigenous to her island home.

"Oh, Shaun, it's beautiful!"

"I thought you'd like it. Hold on a sec," he said, heading toward a nearby kiosk that displayed headgear and assorted souvenirs. "You need a hat."

"I never wear hats. How about a visor?"

"That's not much shade."

"I'll stand in your shade if I need to," Delia said teasingly. "I practically live on the beach most of the year. I think I can take a little Illinois sunshine."

"Okay, okay. Just trying to help."

"How about you? You didn't bring your Murphy Woodworkers cap, either."

"I'll be fine."

"Nope. If I have to wear a hat, so do you."

"Are you always this difficult?"

Delia laughed. "No. Sometimes I'm much worse. Now, what color do you like?"

"Black," Shaun said.

"The guys in the black hats are always the bad guys, Murphy. You need a white one. Definitely a white one."

"Does that mean you think I'm one of the good guys?"

"Absolutely."

She chose a bright yellow visor that matched her T-shirt while Shaun compromised on a red baseball cap. While he was paying for their hats she wandered to the next booth and bought a disposable camera.

As he handed her the visor he eyed her purchase. "What's that for?"

"The butterflies," she said, hoping he wouldn't press her further. She really did intend to take photos in the butterfly house. She also wanted a concrete remembrance of her time with Shaun. Whether he objected or not, she was determined to snap some candid photos of him. Those pictures might be a poor substitute for the real thing in the years to come but they'd be better than nothing, which is what she'd had for the past twelve years. Sadly, everything had happened so fast the day of their wedding they hadn't thought to have even one picture made and she'd always been sorry for that oversight.

"Where to first?" Shaun asked.

"This is your party. You tell me."

He nodded toward the camera in her hand. "Well,

since you're ready for the butterflies, how about starting there?"

"Fine."

Delia was glad she'd brought her sunglasses. Between the glasses darkening her eyes and the visor shading them, she was able to hide her roiling emotions. It was one thing to want a souvenir of her time with Shaun and quite another to reveal how important it was to her.

She lagged back. "Stand over there by the door and I'll take a picture of it."

"Why don't you let me take your picture there, instead?"

"I asked you first."

When he reached for the cardboard camera, Delia held it out of reach so he leaned closer to try to grab it.

She whirled, shielding it with her body the way a basketball player guards the ball from an opponent. Shaun faked to one side, then made a grab for the camera with his other hand.

Delia squealed "No!" and ran.

Shaun was relentless in his pursuit.

They were both laughing as they dodged and parried like children. Delia whirled, ducked around a tree and took a quick step. Momentum nearly carried her into an older couple who were approaching on the path, arm in arm.

Delia put on the brakes so quickly she would have fallen if Shaun hadn't caught her up at the last moment. She laughed. "Oops! Sorry."

The elderly woman grinned. "No problem, dear. I love to see young people enjoying themselves. My husband and I always buy a season pass. We come here all the time. It's wonderful exercise, although we don't usually wrestle. We mostly walk."

"Yes, ma'am." Delia felt her cheeks burning with well-earned embarrassment.

"What were you two tussling about?" the woman asked.

"I wanted to take his picture and the big lug was arguing with me," Delia replied.

When Shaun said "She started it," she jammed her elbow into his ribs and gave him a look of mock disgust.

"Here. Give me the camera and I'll take your picture together," the friendly woman said.

"Oh, I wouldn't want you to go to the trouble."

"Nonsense, girl. You and your husband just stand over there by those pretty flowers and leave the rest to me."

Delia blinked rapidly. Her eyes began to swim with unshed tears behind her dark glasses. Husband? Did she and Shaun really look and act married, or was it a simple case of wishful thinking on the part of their new acquaintance?

Shaun shepherded her to the spot indicated and pulled her to his side with his arm around her shoulders.

"You make a lovely couple," the woman said, sighting through the view finder. "Smile!"

Delia smiled from reflex but her heart was far

from joyful. Being this close to Shaun and having been mistaken for a couple was tearing her apart.

"Advance the film and take one more, will you?" Shaun called pleasantly.

The older woman complied and raised the camera again. Delia didn't have a clue why Shaun had asked for a second picture until he put two fingers under her chin, tilted her face toward him and gently kissed her.

"Perfect!" the amateur photographer said.

Delia agreed completely.

She melted into his embrace and returned his kiss with every fiber of her being. *Perfect?* No, she mused, barely breathing. Shaun's kiss was more than perfect. It was as beautiful as a sunrise, as soft as a rose petal and as inspiring as "The Hallelujah Chorus."

"Angels and ministers of grace, defend us," she quoted silently, remembering *Hamlet,* then turned it into a prayer for divine help. *Lord, please save me from myself.*

That was enough to bring her back to her senses and allow her to offer token resistance.

Smiling bravely she leaned away from Shaun and felt his hold slacken. Instead of speaking to him she turned to the other woman and thanked her as she reclaimed the camera.

"No problem, dear. Enjoy the zoo."

"Thanks. We will." *But not nearly as much as I enjoyed that kiss,* she added to herself. *Boy, did I!*

She huffed in self-derision. At this rate she might

as well throw herself to the alligators and get it over with because she was definitely about to self-destruct.

Shaun was ready to kick himself. He knew better than to get too near Delia, let alone kiss her again. Every sane thought told him to ignore the pull he felt toward her. But there was a contrary bent to his personality that kept insisting he had to press her, to push her, until she told him the truth about her motives.

Would he like what he heard, assuming she did eventually decide to confess? He doubted it. Enough honesty had already emerged from her subconscious to make him wary.

To begin with, her identity was still tied up in the Blanchard family. Oh, she might think she'd gained her independence from Ronald and the rest of her kin but she hadn't. She never would. She was a product of her upbringing just as he was the result of all the history that had gone before in his life. History that had left scars.

For a long time he'd believed that his biggest scar was from his failed marriage. Now that he could look back with more objectivity he could see that losing Delia had merely set him up for everything else that had happened. It had driven him from Stoneley into the military and that had led to the fatal accident that had left him with both literal and figurative scars.

He couldn't blame her directly but he couldn't

overlook her part in the tragedy, either. It was as if she had been the force of gravity that had started his roll down a steep hill and the death of his army buddies had been the crash at the bottom—resulting in memories he'd been trying to escape ever since.

It would be nice if he could blame God instead of Delia or stop shouldering so much of the responsibility himself, Shaun thought. The trouble was, in order to blame God he had to believe in Him in the first place, to give Him the credit for blessing him with the good times as well as shepherding him through the bad.

Shaun wasn't ready to do that again. He'd prayed his heart out when he and Delia had been forced apart by her father and again when he'd been waiting with his unit for the army medics to arrive. What good had any of it done? He wasn't patient the way she was. He wasn't willing to wait a lifetime for an answer to prayer. If God had *really* cared about their marriage, He'd have intervened to help them preserve it years ago, when it had counted.

They stayed so busy, saw so much, the day passed in a blur. By the time Delia crawled back into the SUV late in the afternoon she was more than ready to sit down.

She was still awed by the beauty they'd beheld in the butterfly house. Though not many of the butterflies had emerged from their chrysalises this early in the spring, she'd managed to use up the rest of the film taking pictures of the glorious foliage inside the greenhouse.

"Whew! What a day." She flashed Shaun an appreciative smile. "Thanks for suggesting it."

"You're welcome. Would you like to grab dinner on the way back to the hotel or freshen up first and then go out?"

A few hours ago, Shaun had extended their stay at the hotel for one more night since the outing at the zoo had tired them out. They planned to get a good night's rest and make the trek back to Stoneley in the morning.

Delia settled into the seat and sighed. "Neither. I'm running out of clean clothes to change into and I don't think I can eat another bite, either. I'm stuffed."

"Must be because of the last corn dog."

"Or the two before it," she said, chuckling. "Or maybe the cotton candy."

"That, too." Shaun's smile warmed her far more than the sweatshirt she had purchased at the gift shop when the temperature had dropped.

"I'm really not a bit hungry," she insisted. "But if you are, I'll be glad to keep you company while you eat."

"No. I'm not hungry, either. I just didn't want you to think you had to sit in your room and scarf down more candy bars."

"Can't. I ate 'em all," she said with a rueful smirk. "That's what I should have bought at the gift shop. Candy."

"How about some fresh fruit, instead?"

She arched her eyebrows expressively. "What's with you, Murphy? Do you moonlight for the dietary police or something?"

"No. I'm just trying to take good care of you."

"Why?" Delia visualized him saying it was because he was madly in love with her.

Instead, he said, "Because you don't seem to care about doing it yourself."

"I do okay."

"Oh, sure. Not only do you eat like you have a death wish, you tell me you like to swim in thirty-foot swells with sharks and poisonous jellyfish. Does that sound sensible to you?"

"Perfectly."

"Well, it doesn't to me."

Crossing her arms in a defensive posture, Delia hunkered down in the car seat and withdrew from him emotionally. Shaun was doing it again—sounding way too much like her ultracontrolling father. To listen to Shaun, a person would think all her choices were wrong and all her decisions stank. Why, she couldn't even be trusted to feed herself adequately, could she?

But that wasn't the worst of it. He'd alienated her the minute he'd attacked her beloved surfing career. No wonder she kept having doubts about him. Surfing was her life. Her passion. Riding the breakers gave her a sense of freedom that had been elusive until she'd accidentally found her calling in the warm ocean waves.

Thank goodness she'd found out how negative Shaun felt about her surfing before she got romantically involved with him.

Phooey, she thought, biting her lower lip. She might not be involved with Shaun the way she used to be but her heart was already long gone.

Well, that couldn't be helped. She'd get over him. She'd done it before and she'd do it again.

"Oh, yeah?" she muttered, thoroughly disgusted with herself. "Yeah."

Shaun glanced at her. "What did you say?"

Delia pulled a face. "Nothing. I was just talking to myself."

"And answering?"

She nodded and grimaced. "Yes. And answering. I suppose that makes you think I'm as crazy as the rest of my family."

To her further consternation, Shaun enjoyed a subdued chuckle before he said, "No, honey. You have a long, long way to go before you'll be *that* far gone."

ELEVEN

Shaun could tell that the closer they got to Stoneley, the more tightly wound Delia became. She had chatted some their first day on the road home but by the second day she was either out of words or out of incentive to talk.

He couldn't blame her. If their roles had been reversed he doubted he'd have been very forthcoming, either. She had a lot on her plate right now.

They broke into Maine on Highway 2 late in the afternoon. "It won't be long now," Shaun said.

Delia sighed. "No. I suppose not."

"Want to stop for dinner or keep going?"

"Keep going," she answered soberly. "The sooner I get all this sorted out, the happier I'll be."

"Have you decided what you're going to do first?"

"Kind of." Delia shrugged and managed a smile as she glanced at him. "I've been going over and over everything in my mind. It's still confusing, though."

"Maybe it would help to talk about it." Waiting

for her to speak, Shaun forced himself to remain quiet even though it seemed to be taking her forever to make up her mind.

Finally, she nodded. "Okay. Maybe you're right." She pushed herself fully upright and rested her left knee on the seat so she could partially turn to talk to him. "We know that my mother is probably alive. At least she was a month or so ago when she phoned her parents."

"The Halls."

"Right. And then she disappeared before they could join her at their place in California."

"We can thank Erik Evans for that."

"Right again. Which is where Aunt Genie comes in. She had Mother kidnapped and then drugged her so she could take her somewhere else and hide her."

"Evans thought she was taking Trudy back to Westside Medical Retreat." Shaun paused. "Are we sure she didn't?"

"We're sure. If Dr. Brooks had been lying he'd have told his staff to keep some of the records from us and he didn't do that. He told them to bring everything. Remember? We both heard him."

"And he was never out of our sight so he couldn't have countermanded that order."

"That's right. Plus, he was definitely surprised and upset that Genie was dead."

"No kidding," Shaun agreed. "They must have had a long-standing relationship for him to have been involved with both Genie and your mother for so many years."

Delia nodded thoughtfully. "That's true. My mother was his patient for nearly half her life. That is so sad. I can't imagine how mixed-up she must be by now."

"She was well enough to make her way to California and look up Juliet's father after she escaped from Westside," Shaun reminded her. "Which means she wasn't a total basket case—no offense intended."

"None taken. What has me stumped is where Mother is now. I mean, if Genie stashed her, why hasn't she surfaced now that Genie is out of the picture?"

"Beats me. Do you really think the Halls are involved?"

"Because of Cymbeline? Maybe. I'm still not positive they set up the corporation just to fund my mother's hospitalization but they're certainly at the top of my suspect list."

"Is that where you plan to start? Questioning them, I mean?"

Delia pressed her lips into a thin line and shook her head. "I'm not sure. I think the first thing I'm going to do is try a computer search for Cymbeline on Google."

"You'll probably turn up Shakespeare's plays, instead."

"Probably. But I found the address to Genie's New York condo on the Internet. It's amazing what you can learn if you stick with it."

"What about the rest of your family? Are you going to involve them?"

"I'd rather not," Delia said, "although I know my sisters will want to help." She paused and gazed meaningfully at Shaun before she added, "I'd appreciate it if you'd come with me when I confront my grandparents."

"Why me?"

"Because you can be more objective. I'm afraid, if they do confess, I'll be so upset I won't be rational."

Shaun tried to lift her mood. "You want me to use my martial arts moves on them if they don't talk?"

To his relief, Delia grinned. "Knock it off, Murphy. I'm trying to be serious here."

"Maybe a bit too serious," he countered. "It sounds to me like you're borrowing trouble."

That brought a cynical chuckle. "Hah! In my family we don't have to borrow trouble, it shows up on its own." She sobered. "You know, I can't help wondering if all this grief can't be laid at Grandfather Howard's doorstep. He has a legacy of backstabbing and double-dealing that goes all the way back to his youth. Look at what happened to Aunt Winnie."

Puzzled, Shaun frowned. "Your Aunt Winnie? What's wrong with her?"

"Nothing, now. But Howard ruined her chances for happiness with Tate Connelly when she was much younger. They were head over heels in love many years ago, but my grandfather used his power and influence to rip them apart. Thanks to Tate's nephew Brandon and my sister Juliet, Winnie and Tate have finally started seeing each other again."

Shaun shook his head and blew out a noisy breath. "There you go again. You've lost me. Maybe I will need that program of characters and their histories that you promised, after all."

"Naw, you'll get used to it. Hang around Blanchard manor long enough and it will all start to make sense."

He concentrated on his driving instead of offering a reply. He didn't see any reason to be blunt with Delia and tell her he hoped to never again set foot in that miserable house she used to call home. The door repair was finished…and he was finished with the Blanchards.

Except for one, he added, gritting his teeth. Delia had asked for his help once more and he'd given it. But after he'd accompanied her to confront the Halls, he was done.

Might as well count on that, he told himself. After all, when Delia was through needing him she probably wouldn't give him a second thought. She'd escape to Hawaii the way she always did and leave Maine and its problems far behind. That had been her pattern for years and he couldn't imagine she'd change it.

In a way, he envied her ability to walk away from conflict. The part that hurt was the ease with which she'd walked away from him and their marriage.

Letting her mind wander as she took her turn behind the wheel of the SUV, Delia wondered what else Shaun would have to say if she told him about the close scrapes her sisters had endured lately. Of course, in a tight-knit community like Stoneley some of those facts were already common knowledge but since Shaun hadn't been back in town very long, he probably didn't know the half of it. And when he did find out all that had been happening to the Blanchards he'd most likely be more than thankful to no longer be related, even by marriage.

She viewed herself as the most normal of her siblings but that wasn't saying much. Miranda, the oldest of her sisters, was agoraphobic and prone to panic attacks. Bianca was painfully shy in spite of her successful legal career. Rissa was clinically depressed and, after coming face-to-face with the masked murderer who'd killed her aunt in cold blood, had erroneously believed that she was losing her mind. In the traumatic aftermath of the murder she had barely escaped being the victim of violent crime. Portia had almost lost her life in a botched kidnapping and Juliet had been poisoned. What a family!

What a family to become a part of, Delia added sadly as they drove into Stoneley. No wonder Shaun was trying so hard to keep his distance. He must count their dissolved marriage among his biggest blessings. Not only was her family background filled with turbulence and misfortune, she'd chosen a career that put her in danger over and over, as he'd so cavalierly reminded her. Where she saw freedom and excitement, Shaun saw unnecessary hazards.

If they had still been married he would undoubtedly have tried to stop her from following her dream of surfing competitively and perhaps their marriage would have failed, anyway. It wasn't a pleasant thought but it did help her cope with the feelings of deep loss that kept darkening her normally optimistic outlook.

"A penny for your thoughts?" he said, rousing her from her reverie.

Delia shook her head and managed a slight smile. "Not for a million dollars."

"That bad, huh?"

"No. Just private." She changed the subject. "We're almost there. I'll drop you at your dad's."

"Want me to get the truck and follow you home? Make sure you get there all right?"

"Of course not."

"You don't have to snap at me."

"I didn't snap. I just don't see why you keep inferring that I can't take care of myself. I've been doing it for years."

"Except for the times when I rescued you."

"That was different. Erik Evans isn't going to bother me again."

"No, but you are going back to that big old house where strange things keep happening."

Delia huffed. "No stranger than usual. I grew up there, remember? Besides, I'm not staying long."

"What about your mother? Aren't you going to hang around Stoneley long enough to figure out what happened to her?"

"I'd like to but I really can't. I only have one

regular employee at my surf shop and I'm the resident expert. If I'm not there to teach, I may as well close the doors." She pulled a face. "Besides, Mother has been gone for most of my life. I can't afford to spend another twenty-plus years searching for her with no guarantee I'll ever find her."

"I suppose that is logical."

"Unfortunately."

"So, you'll be leaving soon?"

"As soon as we visit the Halls and make sure we're not missing something there."

She could tell by Shaun's strained expression that he was sorry he'd promised to go with her.

He scrubbed his hands over his face and raked his fingers through his thick, dark hair before heaving a sigh. "Okay. Say when and I'll come pick you up."

"That won't be necessary," Delia replied. "I'll let you know when and where the meeting will be after I get it all arranged. You can meet me there."

"Are you afraid of me, Dee?" he asked, his voice so full of unspoken emotion that it made every one of her nerve endings tingle.

Her head snapped around. "Don't be silly."

Shaun was the only person she had ever permitted to shorten her name and hearing him do it for the first time in years sent an additional shiver up her spine. This whole mess was getting way out of hand. She might not be able to control her family or anyone else but she could control herself. And by doing that, she could limit her exposure to Shaun. It didn't help that she craved his companionship to a depth she couldn't begin to understand. All she had to go on was her gut-level certainty that she had to get away from him and stay away, at all costs.

So why had she asked him to accompany her to confront her grandparents? Because there was no one else whose good sense and honesty she trusted more in that particular situation. Besides, she wasn't about to involve her sisters or Aunt Winnie and place them in a difficult social position. They would most likely have to interact with the Halls on a regular basis, while she'd be safely out of reach on Oahu. If her probing of her grandparents' finances didn't go well, Delia didn't want the others to suffer for her lack of discretion.

She chanced a sidelong glance at Shaun as she approached his father's shop. Although he wasn't looking at her there was still a powerful aura about him that shook her to the core. He'd faced front, folded his arms across his broad chest and was pretending to pay no attention to her.

How did she know he wasn't really ignoring her? The same way she knew when there was a shark in the area where she was paddling her board. She felt the undercurrent of risk, the sense of heightened awareness. Call it a sixth sense, or even divine intervention, but Delia knew better than to ignore niggling warnings like that.

It wasn't a question of believing that Shaun presented the same kind of danger a hungry shark might. Sharks were a passing hazard at best. Shaun was an ever-present challenge to both her heart and mind. She wanted…she *needed* to be near him.

Now that she'd had a taste of what it was like to enjoy his companionship again, she knew it would be much more difficult to go back to her old life, her solitary ways. The men she had dated since moving to Oahu had seemed so inconsequential and lacking that she'd never wanted to take those other relationships past the casual acquaintance stage. Now, she knew why.

Delia blinked rapidly, hoping to clear her head and banish the enlightenment she'd just experienced. Clearly, no other man had captured her heart because no other man had even begun to measure up to Shaun Murphy.

Such a simple truth. And yet such a sad one.

Delia wasn't looking forward to the inquisition she knew she'd face the moment she entered Blanchard manor. To her relief, only Winnie noted her late arrival.

They shared a brief hug, then Delia asked, "Is Father home?"

"No. He's gone to the hospital."

"Is Grandfather worse?"

"No, no. Come up to my suite. We'll have tea and I'll tell you all about it while you fill me in on your trip." Winnie patted Delia's hand and led the way up the stairs to her private, second-floor apartment.

That suggestion suited Delia. She'd always preferred the atmosphere of love and peace in Aunt Winnie's private wing of the enormous house. Winnie's sitting room was elegant but not ostentatious and the ocean view from her sunporch was stunning, even in bad weather.

Moreover, there was a sense of sanctuary in those rooms. There always had been. When the sisters returned to Stoneley, for whatever reasons, they seemed to congregate there more than anywhere else. When they had been children and frightening storms had reminded them of the night their mother had disappeared, they had fled to Winnie for refuge, knowing she would take them in and comfort them with soft words, warm hugs and heartfelt prayers.

In a way, we're still doing that, Delia reasoned. It was good to have a safe port in a storm even if that storm had nothing to do with the weather outside.

As Delia made herself comfortable on the settee she heard Winnie speaking into the intercom. "We'll take tea for two in my sitting room, Sonya. Have Andre make some finger sandwiches and bring us a nice dessert, too."

Delia smiled. Good thing Shaun wasn't here to object to her diet. She focused her smile on her beloved aunt as the older woman joined her. "Thank you. I could eat a little. Sorry I got here too late for supper."

"We haven't kept to much of a schedule since Father's hospitalization," Winnie said, referring to Howard. "He was very sick. We almost lost him."

"Miranda told me he was stable and improving every time I phoned."

"By that time, I imagine he was." Winnie folded her hands gracefully in her lap. "I probably shouldn't tell you this but I think it's only fair that all you girls know. The police suspect that your grandfather's overdose was not unintentional after all. They're pretty sure he was deliberately poisoned."

"What?" Delia leaned closer and laid her hand over Winnie's clasped fingers. They were icy cold. "What makes them think that?"

"A combination of things. There weren't many potassium pills gone when they checked his prescription bottles so they doubt he mistakenly made himself ill the way they'd initially thought. Their conclusion is that his overdose had to have occurred on purpose."

"But who would do such a thing?"

"A better question is, who had access?" Winnie said.

"Besides the family, you mean?"

Winnie sighed and shrugged. "As much as it pains me to say it, I think the police are including the family."

"They wouldn't! Not with Portia and Rissa both planning to marry members of the department."

"You can't blame Mick or Drew," Winnie cautioned. "We certainly wouldn't expect them to try to protect anyone who was guilty."

"Of course not. But there must be another explanation. Who else had access to Grandfather Howard's room the day he got so sick?"

"Ah, there's where it gets interesting," Winnie said. "Your father and I were having lunch in the dining room with his executive assistant, Barbara

Sanchez, when Alannah Stafford barged in and started screaming at him. She said some really dreadful things. The noise brought Sonya and Andre out of the kitchen. Peg, too."

Delia's brow knit, remembering. "That's right. Miranda told me Peg wasn't with Grandfather when he was taken ill."

"No one was. But that's getting ahead of my story."

Winnie paused as Sonya entered and placed the tea tray on the low table beside the settee. It was all Delia could do to hold her questions until the maid had finished and left the room.

"Go on," Delia said, reaching for a delicate sandwich and a napkin. "What happened after that? I want to know everything."

"It was dreadful," Winnie said. "Barbara managed to get Alannah calmed down a bit, then took her upstairs to the powder room so she could speak with her in private. In the meantime, your father was calling his lawyers about getting a restraining order."

"That's not a big surprise."

"No, it isn't. While he was busy doing that, Peg decided to check on Howard. She said she wanted to make sure the awful commotion hadn't awakened him. He was resting comfortably so she came back to finish her meal in the kitchen with Sonya."

"Could Alannah have done something to Grandfather?"

"It is possible, I suppose. Barbara left her alone for a few minutes to go speak with one of the servants about needing fresh fingertip towels. When she went back into the powder room, Alannah wasn't there. She'd apparently decided to leave quietly and had used the back stairs, although no one saw her go."

"Could she have sneaked up to Grandfather's room without being noticed?"

"Nobody can see how, given the limited amount of time, although nothing is impossible I suppose. After Barbara came down and told your father Alannah was missing, we all went out to the front porch and saw her car racing away. He was so upset he refused to eat another bite. He and Barbara left shortly after that to go back to the office."

"And Grandfather was ill when Sonya took him his tea a little while later?"

"Yes. The poor woman was frantic. She buzzed the kitchen and told Peg to come up right away. The rest, you know."

Delia shook her head as she mulled over the confusing story. "I still don't see why it couldn't have been accidental. Grandfather is always so confused."

"Yes, but he can't just snap his fingers and make prescription medicine appear out of thin air, although if he could, that might explain those tablets that were found in the library after your Aunt Genie's unfortunate end."

"Those were supposed to be his, weren't they? Wasn't that why the police suspected him?"

"Originally. Now, there's more to it than that."

"I don't believe this. What else can there possibly be?" Delia asked incredulously.

"Well, remember that detective Bianca hired

shortly after my birthday? His death is being ques-
tioned, too." She sighed. "I know it was only a few
months ago, but it seems like an eternity since then."

"Bianca's detective? You mean Garrett McGraw?
I thought the investigation into his crash was completed. Wasn't the thug who kidnapped Mick's
daughter implicated in the crime?

"So, we'd thought. But the police now suspect he
might have been framed and that the real murderer
is still out there. Bianca was very upset when she
heard the probe was ongoing, as you can imagine,
especially after the toxicologists found high levels
of Xanax and alcohol in McGraw's system." Winnie
shuddered.

"A tranquilizer?"

"An antidepressant, I believe. Mick told Portia
that Xanax can be lethal when mixed with alcohol."

"Poor Bianca. I imagine she feels awful."

"Yes. I'm thankful she's in Boston, away from all
these terrible goings-on. And I'll be even happier
when you're on your way back to Hawaii." She smiled
wistfully. "Although I shall miss you. Terribly."

"I'll miss you, too," Delia said, patting the older
woman's hands.

"So, tell me about your adventure. When you
called, you told Miranda you were going on to
Chicago, I believe."

"Yes. Shaun and I caught up to Erik Evans in
upstate New York. He was ransacking Aunt Genie's
condominium."

"Oh, dear. I'm thankful you had Shaun with you."

"I admit he was handy, although I did have to help him a little." She couldn't help grinning as she remembered that encounter. "We actually worked pretty well together."

"My, my."

"Oh, no. Don't look at me like that, Aunt Winnie. There was nothing personal about it. We just seemed to balance each other out, that's all, especially when it came to questioning people."

"What did you find out in Chicago? Did you go to the same hospital Bianca and Leo visited?"

"Yes. And it was every bit as depressing as Bianca had said. But I had the added advantage of knowing what had happened to Aunt Genie. You should have seen the reaction I got when I mentioned her name! That Dr. Brooks almost keeled over. I'd have felt sorrier for him if he hadn't been responsible for keeping Mother prisoner."

Winnie frowned. "I don't understand. Why would he be so upset about Genie?"

"Because he'd been having a fling with her for years. I think that's why he was able to ignore medical ethics and his guilty conscience for so long. When we told him Genie was gone for good, he confessed everything."

"Oh, my. Does he know where Trudy went?"

"Unfortunately, no." Delia sighed and shook her head. "But I did manage to come away with one clue. Have you ever heard of Cymbeline Corporation?"

"Cymbeline? You mean like Shakespeare's play?"

"Yes. It's spelled exactly the same way. Aunt Genie had been drawing on a Cymbeline Corporation account to pay Mother's hospital bills."

"How odd."

"I agree. That's why, tomorrow, I'm going to pay a call on Eleanor and Stanley. I want to watch their faces when I bring it up."

"You think *they're* involved?"

"I don't know," Delia said firmly, "but I'm sure going to find out."

"You're not going to face them all by yourself?"

"No," Delia said, her tone softening as she thought of Shaun. "I won't be alone."

TWELVE

Shaun arrived at the Coastal Inn just before three the following afternoon. He wasn't supposed to meet Delia there until three-thirty but he didn't want to be late.

The inn was the kind of upscale, pricey place he'd have imagined any relatives of the Blanchards would choose so he wasn't surprised when Delia had told him her maternal grandparents were staying there. He could certainly understand why they wouldn't want to be housed at Blanchard manor, instead. If ever there was a place with a stifling, morbid atmosphere, the Blanchard estate was it.

The Coastal Inn wasn't so bad in comparison, Shaun thought, climbing out of his work truck, straightening his brown corduroy blazer over his black turtleneck and starting to circle the Victorian structure in preparation for meeting Delia. He'd gone to the rear where employees parked and deliveries were made rather than chance being asked to move his well-used vehicle because it didn't fit the posh image the inn wanted to create for its guests.

There had been a time, long ago, when he'd wished he could take Delia to the Coastal Inn for a fancy meal but he'd abandoned that dream when he'd found out what it would have cost. On the wages he'd been making in those days he'd have been lucky to be able to afford one dessert and two forks!

Since then, having a lot of discretionary money had ceased to be as important to him. Delia was right about one thing in that regard. Her family's wealth had *not* brought them happiness.

He climbed the curving front stairs of the inn and sauntered along the covered porch that graced its front and sides. The aroma of salt air, warmed by afternoon sun, was mixed with the sweetness of roses and honeysuckle twining up a trellis at the east end.

Shaun paused and shaded his eyes. He had to admit that the sea view from the porch was magnificent—almost as grand as the land and seascape from the grounds of Blanchard manor. He recalled being impressed the few times he'd strolled there with Delia.

She'd been eager and energetic in those days. Young. Full of mischief. When she'd led him closer to the edge of the bluff he'd naturally kept hold of her hand.

"Don't get so close," Shaun recalled warning her as he'd tried to pull her back.

Delia had giggled and danced away, teasing. "Scaredy cat. What are you afraid of?"

Losing you, Shaun had thought. He'd said something macho instead. "I'm not afraid of anything. I just don't think you should be fooling around so close to the edge, that's all. It might give way."

"Don't worry," she had replied. "I'm not ready to go to heaven quite yet." She had sobered. "Although I would like to see my mother again."

Shaun smiled as he pictured her sweet face and stared off into the distance, daydreaming. Maybe she would get the chance to actually see her mother soon. If there was anything he could do to help her, he'd give it his best. Delia and Trudy deserved to be reunited, to get to know each other again.

He'd be willing to literally trade years of his life if he thought it would bring his own mother back. She and his dad had had a very special relationship; a rare and precious understanding that had often let them communicate without words.

Though his mother had regularly taken Shaun with her to Sunday school she had never preached to his dad. Yet, once she was gone, it was as if her spirit had finally drawn Ian into church and given him comfort there.

That kind of restful assurance was one thing Shaun had never understood. To him, church was a reminder of his sins, of his failures, and he didn't see any reason to put himself through that kind of gut-wrenching trauma at all, let alone do it on a weekly basis.

The warm sun on his face caused him to squint, made his eyes water. He knuckled away the moisture. Dwelling in the past was idiotic. Wishing wouldn't bring his mother back and it couldn't change the result of the accident that had cost him so many of his army buddies, either.

Still, he supposed it wouldn't hurt to fall back on what he'd learned at his mother's side and say a little prayer once in a while. Like maybe now.

With his back to the inn and its guests he leaned against one of the carved porch columns, faced the ocean below the bluff and closed his eyes.

Lord, it's been a long time, he prayed silently. *I don't know what to ask or how to go about this but please help Delia. Help me to take care of her. To do and say the right things. To be there for her.*

Overwhelmed with emotion, Shaun brushed at his eyes as he scanned the approach to the inn. A little, scratched, compact car had just pulled up to the valet parking attendant and stopped.

She was here.

Delia looked at the covered porch of the Coastal Inn. Her breath caught. Shaun! He'd come, just as she'd asked. After the gruff way he'd sounded when she'd phoned to give him the details, she hadn't been positive he'd actually show up for the meeting.

There was no way she could have stifled her joy if she'd wanted to. Grinning as if she were about to meet her best friend, which was exactly what she was about to do, she smoothed the hem of her short-sleeved, teal sweater over her softly draped navy skirt, slung the strap of her purse over her shoulder and started up the stairs.

Shaun waited at the top and held out his hand.

Delia took it, gladly. "I'm so nervous. How do I look?"

"Wonderful."

"Thank you. You're not so bad, yourself. That's a nice jacket."

"It was the fanciest thing I had. I hope it's good enough for this place. I don't want to embarrass you."

Delia laughed quietly as Shaun held the door for her. "I usually go to restaurants that barely require shoes, so don't worry about me. Besides, I think you look great."

"Thanks."

She led the way to the front desk and smiled a greeting at the clerk. "Good afternoon. Will you please tell Mr. and Mrs. Stanley Hall that Delia Blanchard is here. They're expecting me."

"Yes, ma'am. Mr. Hall told me you'd be arriving. He said to ask you to go on up. Room 212. It's on your right at the top of the stairs."

Delia turned to Shaun. "Well, here goes nothing."

"I'm right with you," he said, taking her arm.

"Guess it's too late to chicken out, huh?"

"You can do this. *We* can do this."

"I know. I just hate conflict. If I accuse them of being behind Cymbeline Corporation and they're not, we're all going to feel awful." She let Shaun shepherd her up the sweeping staircase.

"If I were them and people were doing all they could to find my missing daughter, I'd be grateful no matter what."

"Thanks." Delia gazed at him, marveling at how much stronger she felt with him at her side. The butterflies in her stomach were still fluttering like mad but they were no longer threatening to escape and bring her meager lunch along for the ride.

They paused at the door of room 212. "Well, this is it," she said, raising her hand to knock.

Before she could, the door was jerked open and Eleanor greeted her with a tight hug that left her breathless.

"Thank you for agreeing to see me," Delia said.

Eleanor's green eyes misted. "Oh, my dear. You have no idea how glad we are that you called. Aren't we, Stanley?"

"Delighted," he called from inside the suite. "Don't make the poor girl stand out there, Eleanor. Invite her in."

The older woman eyed Shaun as she stepped back and gestured with a sweep of her arm. "Please, do come in. Both of you."

"Eleanor, Stanley, this is my...friend, Shaun Murphy," Delia said, smiling nervously as they entered. "He went with me to Chicago while we checked on Mother's past and I thought..."

"Of course, of course," the older man said. He extended his hand and pumped Shaun's in magnanimous greeting. "We're glad to have you both. Eleanor's been pacing all morning, waiting for your visit. Now maybe she'll settle down before she wears a path in the carpet and the hotel charges me to replace it."

Delia studied Shaun's expression, hoping to judge his reaction to her grandparents by what she observed. He removed all doubt when he smiled and said, "I like this branch of your family, Delia."

She had to admit that she did, too. That was why it was so hard to imagine them being a party to holding her mother prisoner.

"I had tea sent up," Eleanor said, gracefully seating herself on the tufted, brocade Victorian sofa. "I hope you don't mind not going down to the dining room. I thought we could get better acquainted if we had a bit of privacy."

"I agree," Delia replied. She took a chair opposite her grandmother but perched on the edge as if ready to flee at a moment's notice.

"Shall I pour?" Eleanor asked.

Delia waved her hand and noticed that it was trembling. "Please. Nothing for me. I—I need to talk to you and I've been so nervous I couldn't possibly eat a thing."

"Now that *is* surprising," Shaun quipped. He stood beside her chair and gently touched her shoulder. "Sorry. Go on. Tell them what we learned. It'll be okay."

The calming effect of his voice, of his touch, helped Delia relate the disturbing details of their encounter with Erik Evans and their subsequent visit to Westside Medical Retreat.

Eleanor dabbed at her eyes as she listened and when Delia spoke about Genie's relationship with the doctor she nodded soberly.

"My Genie was always wild," the older woman said. "We never could understand why she defied us the way she did."

"She had set up a method of payment for my mother's care that has me puzzled," Delia told her. "I—we—thought perhaps you two could shed some light on it." She paused to see if either of her grandparents was going to speak before she went on to ask, "Have you ever heard of Cymbeline Corporation?"

Stanley had been staring out the window and rocking back on forth on his heels and the balls of his feet while he listened. Now, his bushy gray brows knit and he crossed to the sofa to join his wife. "Cymbeline? You mean like the Bard's work?"

"Yes. It was spelled exactly the same. I thought perhaps, since your press was well-known for printing famous literature and Imogen is part of that play's cast, you might have financed Genie that way. You know—because she was named after that character?"

Eleanor's voice was reedy. "You think we had something to do with Trudy's hospitalization?" She reached for her husband's hand.

"You are her parents," Shaun said cautiously.

"Yes, but we would never..." Stanley stopped and cleared his throat. "I take that back. There was a time when we tried to get Genie psychiatric help but she refused to listen to us or to her doctors. If she was connected with this Cymbeline outfit she did it on her own. It had nothing to do with us."

"I believe you," Delia said. "I'm sorry. You can see why I had to ask. I don't really know you and I didn't know what to think."

"Well, now you do," Shaun said, giving her shoulder a pat before stepping away. "I believe them, too. In a way, it's too bad. Now we may never know where that money came from."

Eleanor had begun to weep so Delia knelt at her feet and took her hand. "Please don't cry. I didn't mean to hurt your feelings."

"It's just…so…awful." Eleanor held a handkerchief to her mouth and struggled to speak between sobs.

Stanley agreed by quoting Edgar in *King Lear.* "Yes. 'Let's just tell the truth. This happened. This is sad.' The sister who needed the care kept the healthy one prisoner. If only we'd known. Maybe we could have done something. Intervened. Made Genie tell us the truth."

"I don't understand why my mother never took us to see you," Delia said. "I mean, there were years before she and Father split up that we could have gotten to know you. Why would she act as if you didn't exist?"

Stanley cleared his throat again, more noisily this time. "You don't know?"

Delia's eyes widened. "No."

"Then I suppose it's time someone told you. Trudy always insisted she had to protect Ronald from Howard," Stanley explained. "The old man held the reins of the family business with an iron fist. He hated Trudy and controlled Ronald—except for the one time when your father took a chance and used his trust fund to keep my small press afloat. For that, I shall be eternally grateful.

"You and your sisters were young, innocent children. If Trudy had brought you to meet us and you'd accidentally mentioned it in front of Howard, he probably would have kicked your father out on his ear. Trudy knew how much the business meant to Ronald so she made that sacrifice. So did we. We saw photos, of course. And she told us all about you and the other girls as you grew."

Stanley hesitated and swallowed hard. "Until one day, shortly after she left your father and we thought we might start seeing more of her, she simply stopped contacting us."

Tears filled Delia's eyes. She raised her face to Shaun. He held out his hand, drew her to her feet and took her in his arms.

She didn't want to give in and weep in front of her grandparents but everything seemed to weigh on her until she was unable to continue fighting her emotions. Her father's act of kindness had come at a hefty price. Although she was no closer to finding her mother, her new knowledge of her father's altruism all those years ago did make her see him in a new light. Was it possible that he could one day be that kind of self-sacrificing man again?

Despite this ray of hope, a sense of melancholy settled over her heart. The Blanchards hadn't been a real family, she concluded. With the exception of her sisters and Winnie, they had been individuals who had simply resided in the same cold mansion. No wonder they all seemed to suffer from various types of social dysfunction. It was a wonder any of them even approached normalcy!

Delia's tears flowed in spite of her efforts to stifle them. What must Shaun be thinking? She wouldn't blame him if he was counting his blessings over the annulment of their marriage. Who would want to become part of a family like hers?

Shaun didn't know what to say so he kept silent. Delia's shoulders were shaking. He gently rubbed her back as he held her close.

True to their generational and cultural differences, Stanley was standing behind Eleanor and had merely laid his hands on her shoulders to steady her as she sobbed. Shaun could tell that the older man was fighting tears, too.

Poor Delia. And poor Trudy. He'd grown up an only child but he couldn't imagine Genie being so jealous that she'd imprison her sibling, let alone keep her locked away for so many years. The most astonishing part was that she'd gotten away with it. In any normal family, surely somebody would have sounded an alarm and ended the nightmare before a whole life was wasted.

Delia had been resting her palms on his chest. Now, she gave a faint push and Shaun loosened his hold.

"Better?" he asked.

"I—I want to go," she managed between shaky breaths.

"All right." Arm around her shoulders, Shaun guided her toward the door, then paused to speak to their host and hostess while Delia fished in her purse for a tissue and blew her nose.

"We'll be back when everybody has calmed down," Shaun said. "I promise. In the meantime, if either of you think of any connection to Cymbeline other than Shakespeare, please let us know."

Stanley nodded. "Of course. Take care of our girl."

"I will," Shaun assured him. He meant it. He just didn't know what to do next. Obviously, neither did Delia. He could understand her desire to get away from everybody and everything. He only hoped that desire for solitude included him.

He guided her down the stairs and out the front door then paused on the porch of the inn while she donned dark glasses. "I think I should drive, don't you?"

"I'm perfectly…" Her statement was interrupted by a loud hiccup, followed quickly by a sniffle and capitulation. "Okay. Maybe you're right. You drive. We can come back for my car later."

"Stay right there. I'll get the truck," he said.

Keeping an eye on her to make sure she was going to do as he'd suggested, he strode around the edge of the inn's porch, then broke into a jog once he could no longer see her. The sooner he got her into his truck and out of there, the sooner she'd recover.

If she ever did, he added wryly. He couldn't imagine what must be going through Delia's head right now but it couldn't be good. He hadn't wanted her maternal grandparents to be guilty of conspiracy but it sure would have been easier if they had been. At least then they'd know who, besides Dr. Brooks, had abetted Genie all these years and they could have put that question to rest.

They?

Yes, they. Shaun snorted derisively. He didn't know when he had begun thinking of Delia and himself as a single unit, as a couple, but that's what he was now doing. Her problems were his problems. Her sadness was his. And her eventual triumph, assuming they did locate her mother, was going to be shared, too.

He couldn't picture it any other way.

"I want to go by the factory," Delia said as Shaun chauffeured her past the theater and quaint shops in downtown Stoneley.

His head snapped around. "Blanchard Fabrics? Why?"

"I don't know, exactly. I just have this urge to go there."

"I'd think that would be the last place you'd want to go, considering the state of mind you're in right now."

"I'm okay—although my emotions are all over the place. A part of me is really proud of Father for helping out Stanley and Eleanor all those years ago. Yet, at the same time, it makes me unbearably sad that Mother chose to cut herself off from her parents for Father's sake. I think both my parents made some bad mistakes. That just means they're human. We all are."

"You're a lot more forgiving than I am."

"Not really. I'm at the end of my rope, Shaun. I've been so angry and so confused for so long I guess I'm tired of fighting. Father is Father. He is what he is, even if I don't respect the man he's become."

Pensive, she sighed and stared out the window at the passing scene for a few moments before she added, "My father, like my grandfather, has squandered his happiness while hoarding the earthly riches he thought were important.

Now that he's broken up with Alannah, maybe that means he's seeing the error of his ways."

"Don't you think it's a little late?"

"No. It won't be too late until he takes his last breath," Delia said wisely.

"I disagree. There's too much water under the bridge, as folks say."

The same is true of our relationship, she thought sadly. *That's what you're really trying to tell me, isn't it, Shaun? Well, I understand. And in a way, I agree. The innocence and pure love we once shared has been destroyed beyond repair and there's not a thing either of us can do about it except go on with our lives and learn from the experience, sad as it was.*

Sighing, she forced a smile. "Water under the bridge? Maybe that's why I love the ocean so much.

Water from all the little streams eventually flows into it and is cleansed in the vast, open sea."

"Cleansed of pollution?"

"No, silly. That was an analogy, not science. What I meant was, our petty problems are really nothing when you consider them against the immeasurable distances and beauty of the universe."

"That's not a reference to science, either, is it?"

She shook her head, her smile blossoming. "No. It's more theology. I can't explain why, but I can't look at the sky or the sea without thinking of God. I suspect most people feel that way, even if they choose to deny it. Pastor Greg says there's a God-shaped hole in everyone's soul that needs filling. Some people fill it with God. Others keep searching all their lives and never find peace."

"I know lots of so-called Christians who aren't happy," Shaun countered.

"So do I," Delia said. "Like Father, they're still human, but you never know what they might have been like if they hadn't decided to follow Jesus Christ. I know it's made a difference in my life, even if I haven't been nearly as faithful as I should have."

"What about your grandfather? Howard Blanchard was supposed to have been a pillar of the church at one time. Surely, you aren't trying to tell me that *he's* a true believer."

"I don't know." She sighed. "A couple of my sisters seem to think so but it's not my place to judge. I have enough trouble taking care of my own spiritual life without trying to police someone else's."

She saw Shaun's eyebrows arch before he said, "I suppose you're right. Like they used to say in the army, 'Let God sort 'em out.'"

His statement reminded her of war and gave her sudden chills. "Did you ever kill anyone in battle, Shaun?"

He answered, "No," but judging by the way his hands were gripping the steering wheel and his jaw was clenched, Delia knew there had to be more to it than he was revealing. He had told her about being issued a gun and being taught to shoot. She didn't recall him mentioning actually going into combat but considering the kind of upheaval the world was in these days, he might easily have been deployed.

Clearly, he didn't want to talk about his military service. Well, fine. Let him play the closemouthed, stalwart hero if he wanted. She wasn't going to keep her ideas to herself just because Shaun chose to hide his feelings. He might not appreciate her concern and willingness to help but she certainly appreciated his.

That was why she'd asked him to drive her to Blanchard Fabrics instead of going there later by herself. Though she saw no reason to spell it out for him, she wanted Shaun by her side when she entered the lion's den. Although her faith was getting stronger every day she worked to find her missing mother, she was far from being as close to God as the prophet Daniel had been in the Old Testament.

It took a lot less courage for Delia to ride thirty-foot breakers on a surfboard than it did to simply visit her father's office.

THIRTEEN

Blanchard Fabrics, both the plant and corporate offices, was located in an outlying part of town that was almost exclusively industrial. The redbrick building looked antiquated on the outside but had a modern interior. The factory part of the operation had always been kept up-to-date. When Ronald had finally taken over from Howard, Delia had heard he'd brought in the latest in office technology, too. Juliet had told her that walking in the front door was like stepping forward a full century.

Delia paused at the entrance.

Shaun gently touched her elbow. "Are you okay?"

"Yes. No. I don't know."

"Well, that's definitive."

She had to chuckle. "It was, wasn't it?"

"Care to tell me what we're doing here?"

"I think I was going to face my father and tell him about what we learned from Eleanor and Stanley."

"You're not sure?" Shaun was giving her a lopsided smile and his comical expression made Delia laugh again.

"No, I'm not sure. But then, I come from a family of pretty confused individuals so that shouldn't surprise you."

"Nothing you do surprises me much," Shaun said. His grin spread. "Well, except maybe the stories about swimming with sharks."

"Hah! That's the easy part of my life. Trying to make sense of my relationship to my father is the hard part."

"You don't have to rush things, you know. You could wait till he gets home and talk to him there."

Yes, but then you wouldn't be with me, Delia countered without voicing her thoughts. Instead, she said, "Let's stop and say hello to Juliet first. That should relax me."

"Fine." Shaun pushed open the outer door.

Delia couldn't help but be impressed by the modernization she found inside. "Wow. Juliet wasn't kidding when she said this place had been fixed up."

"Yeah." Shaun leaned close to speak more privately. "Dad would say it's like gilding the lily but personally, I think it's high time Blanchard Fabrics stepped into the future. Stoneley would be in real trouble if this business ever failed."

"I know. Supporting a whole town is an awesome responsibility if you stop and think about it. No wonder Father is so intense about his work." She paused and smiled at Shaun. "Of course, there is the money, too."

"Buckets of it, judging by the way he lives."

"I did have everything I wanted when I was a child."

"Except a mother," Shaun reminded her.

Delia's smile faded. "Yes. Except my mother. Come on. Juliet's cubicle is in marketing. We'll pop in and surprise her."

Juliet jumped out of her chair and greeted Delia with a squeal of delight and a hug. "Come in, come in—if you can find room." She eyed Shaun. "Hi, handsome. You still hanging around my sister?"

Delia gasped and blushed. "Juliet!"

"Just wondered. Seems to me you and Shaun have been spending a lot of extra time together. You won't tell me what's been going on so I figured I'd ask him."

"We're just friends," Shaun said amiably as he shouldered into the cramped space. "Nice little place you have here."

"Cubicle, Sweet Cubicle," Juliet quipped. She swiveled her computer chair and gestured toward it. "Have a seat, Delia. What brings you to beautiful Blanchard Fabrics? We don't make those gaudy Hawaiian prints you love, so I know it can't be that."

"Well, you can't be expected to do everything perfectly this far north," Delia replied. "Actually, we were in town because I just visited our new grandparents."

"Really? How are they? Aunt Winnie has invited them to the house for dinner more than once but they've always made excuses. I'm surprised they welcomed you. They did, didn't they?" She peered at Delia, then frowned at Shaun. "You kind of look like you've been crying."

Delia sighed. "I have. But not because of anything the Halls did. They were wonderful, even after I accused them of helping Genie keep our mother from us."

"You *what*?" The younger girl plunked into the only other chair, ignoring the fact it was draped with fabric swatches. "What made you do that?"

Delia quickly related her conversation with Dr. Brooks and her discovery in the mental hospital financial records.

"So, when I saw the name Cymbeline Corporation," she said in conclusion, "I got the idea that the Halls might be involved because of the Shakespearian connection."

"Cymbeline Corporation?" Juliet's voice was barely a breath.

"Yes. Have you heard of it?"

"For some reason it rings a bell." Scowling, she jumped to her feet. "Change chairs with me so I can use the computer. I want to look something up."

Delia stood shoulder to shoulder with Shaun and watched her youngest sister's fingers fly over the keyboard.

"It was just a couple of weeks ago," Juliet said as she typed. "I probably wouldn't have noticed the name if it hadn't been Shakespearean." She was paging down at a dizzying rate while Delia and Shaun leaned closer and tried to follow what she was doing.

Suddenly, she shouted, "Got it!" and hit the key to display the full file.

Delia was glad Shaun was beside her to steady her

because she began to feel dizzy. The screen blurred. She blinked to clear her vision. She couldn't believe it, yet there it was, for all the world to see.

Cymbeline Corporation was an obscure branch of a well-known parent company. Blanchard Fabrics.

Delia was too shocked to cry. Too furious to speak. She glanced at Shaun and saw the muscles of his beard-shadowed jaw clenching. It was at times like these that his dark, fast-growing beard gave his face an almost sinister aspect. That, and the anger so clearly displayed in the steely blue of his eyes, accentuated his rage.

"Your father again," he whispered hoarsely.

Delia nodded miserably, realizing she'd been a fool to be swayed by her father's one act of kindness all those years ago. Once again, he'd shown his true colors. She reached for Juliet's hand and held it tightly. "We must keep this quiet until we can speak with Father in private. Can you do that?"

The blond girl nodded. "Yes. Of course. I can tell Brandon, can't I? He and I don't have any secrets from each other."

Delia nodded. She was beginning to regain her equilibrium and think more clearly. "By all means. I'll call a family meeting for tonight, after supper." She eyed the computer. "Can you make me a printout of that page? I want something on paper."

"Sure." Juliet printed the information and handed it to her sister.

"Now what?" Shaun asked. "Are you going to go to your father's office?"

"I'm not sure what I should do. As angry as I am, I might say something I'd be sorry for later." She noticed that the paper she held was quivering. "I can wait. I have to wait. My sisters and Aunt Winnie and the Halls have as much right to hear what Father has to say as I do."

She gazed up at him, her emotions totally exposed. "Will you come tonight, too, Shaun?"

"Do you want me to?"

"Yes. Very much. You deserve to hear this."

He nodded solemnly. "All right. What time?"

"Around seven." She scanned the short walls enclosing Juliet's cubicle and realized that, although she hadn't noticed anyone else occupying the adjoining spaces when they'd arrived, someone might be in a position to be listening now.

"Let's go out to your truck so I can use my cell phone in private," Delia said. "After I make a few calls I'll know more." She patted her baby sister on the shoulder. "Will you be all right if we leave you alone?"

"I'm going to Brandon's office. I won't be alone." Juliet stood and hugged Delia. "Thank you."

"For what?"

"For digging until you got to the truth."

"We still don't know exactly what that truth is," Delia cautioned, keeping her voice down. "Father could be innocent."

"Only if Grandfather is solely responsible. Remember, he's been sick for a long time. Even if Cymbeline was his idea, Father has been running this company. He'd surely have noticed a nonproductive drain on the firm. I'm surprised Brandon didn't question it."

"Maybe he did. You can ask him when you see him."

She watched Juliet lay a hand on Shaun's forearm to command his full attention. "Take care of her for us? Please? She's a very special part of our family."

"I will." He pulled Delia to his side, holding her there with a light, supportive touch as he urged her toward the doorway. "Come on. Let's get you out of here before somebody notices you're in the building and tells *Daddy*. I don't imagine you'd appreciate being ambushed before you get your plans worked out."

"Right," Delia said with a slight shiver. "My father is the *last* person I want to see or talk to right now."

Sunlight shining into the pickup truck had overheated the interior so Shaun had rolled down the windows. An ocean breeze ruffled Delia's short hair.

She pushed the button to end her telephone conversation and leaned back against the seat with a sigh. "Well, that's the last one. Bianca's busy in Boston, as I'd thought, so she won't be able to be there tonight. Rissa's in New York so she's out, too. Portia said she'd try to make it. I asked her not to bring her fiancé, Mick Campbell, since he's with the police and I'm not sure exactly what we'll find out."

"Do you think your father is guilty of a crime?"

"It's a distinct possibility."

"You're sure you want me to be there?" Shaun asked.

"Absolutely. You deserve to be. Not only were you involved in my current search, you and I were victims all along."

"We were? How?"

"Think about it, Shaun. I was flighty and confused when I was a teenager, at least partly because of my dysfunctional home life. If I'd had the benefit of my mother's counsel back then, maybe I'd have been smart enough to know I couldn't run away from my problems and I wouldn't have latched on to you and hurt you the way I did." She paused to gather her courage before she added, "I'm sorry, Shaun. I'm so sorry."

"No problem. That was a long time ago."

Delia didn't know what she'd expected him to say but she certainly wasn't ready to hear him shrug off their marriage as if it hadn't mattered. It had taken her years to get over losing him. Apparently, Shaun had not been nearly as devastated. She knew it wasn't right or fair to hold him responsible for being more emotionally resilient than she was but she couldn't help doing it.

A lot of the things that had happened to her and Shaun hadn't been fair, had they? If he was able to easily get over her and go on with his life, more power to him. She just wished she could say the same for herself.

"What about the Halls?" Shaun asked. "You told

Juliet you were going to include them and I didn't hear you call them."

"You're right. But what am I going to say?"

"Well, I wouldn't go into detail about what you suspect the way you did with your sisters. Why not just tell them that you've found some information about Cymbeline and you thought they might like to drop by the house tonight to talk it over?"

"Do you think that's sensible? I mean, Eleanor was already upset over our visit, today. This revelation about Father's involvement may be much harder on her."

"Then let me talk to Stanley for you. He can decide how much his wife can stand."

"Fair enough. But not on the phone. I have to go back to the Coastal Inn to get my car, anyway. We can ask him to come downstairs and you can talk to him then."

"All right."

Delia could tell that Shaun was not thrilled with her decision. She'd have stepped in and relieved him of having to deal with her maternal grandfather if he hadn't been so right about how best to handle the situation. Speaking to Stanley man-to-man was by far the wisest choice. Since Shaun had offered, Delia was going to let him go through with it.

Yes, it was the coward's way out. And, yes, she was not displaying her usual bravado. But she was weary beyond reason. Her mind had been on overload ever since she'd undertaken this quest and her heart was now totally involved, too.

Looking for villains in her own family was only the half of it. Finding love again, where it was not reciprocated, was the other half of the equation.

Delia didn't like the way either situation was working out. If she hadn't felt a duty to her sisters, to her missing mother, and now to her grandparents, she'd have hopped the first plane out of Bangor and headed for the sanctuary that waited for her on Oahu.

Soon, that was exactly what she was going to do.

Shaun gritted his teeth as he stood on the porch of the Coastal Inn and waited for Stanley Hall to join him. He had no idea what he was going to tell the man but he figured something would come to mind. For once, Delia hadn't tried to interfere and he wished she had. This situation was extremely important to her. Shaun didn't want to make things any harder than they already were by saying or doing the wrong thing.

Still, Delia had left, trusting him to approach Stanley alone, so she must feel comfortable with his diplomatic ability. He just hoped he had some of that tact left when he next came face-to-face with Ronald Blanchard.

Stanley burst out the door, spotted him and hurried over. "What's wrong? I had to fib to my wife to get away from her and I don't like doing that. You sounded deadly serious when you called on the house phone. Is Delia all right?"

"She's fine." Shaun shook the older man's hand.

"Thanks for coming down. Delia and I thought it would be best if I briefed you first and let you break the news to your wife."

"Have you found our Trudy?"

"Not yet. But Delia keeps getting closer. She's uncovered a connection between her family and that Cymbeline Corporation we had asked you about earlier."

"What is it?"

"Blanchard Fabrics," Shaun said, pausing to let the information sink in before he went on. Obviously, Stanley was stunned.

"Ronald?" the older man guessed.

"Looks like it. Him, or old Howard. Delia and Juliet think it was probably their father's doing, though. Howard might have set it up but Ronald had to have been the one keeping the whole thing funded."

Stanley sagged back against the exterior wall of the inn and shook his head slowly. "Why?"

"I don't know. The girls have called a family meeting for tonight. Can you and Eleanor be there?"

"Of course. Where and when?"

"At the estate. Around seven. I'll tell Delia to expect you. Ronald doesn't know anything about this yet so keep the details to yourself, will you?"

"I'm going to tell Eleanor."

"We assumed you'd want to," Shaun said with evident empathy. "That's why I'm here. It would be best if she were prepared ahead of time, don't you think?"

Stanley continued to nod. "Yes." He held out his

hand and shook Shaun's with gusto. "I don't know how to thank you, son."

"Getting Delia's family back on track will be all the thanks I need."

"You and my granddaughter. What's the story there?"

"No story," Shaun said. He took a deep breath and blew it out with a puff. "There used to be, but there isn't anything going on now."

"I wouldn't be so sure," Stanley replied. "I saw the way you two looked at each other, the way you both seemed to rely on each other for support when you were up in our suite."

"Delia only needs me to help her through this mess she's gotten into regarding her mother," Shaun said. "Things will be settled soon and she'll head back to Hawaii without a second thought."

The older man chuckled quietly and clapped Shaun on the shoulder. "She may go back, as you say, but I doubt it'll be without plenty of second thoughts."

"It won't matter." Shaun was adamant. "She married me in the first place, when we were kids, as a way to escape her unhappy home life. She told me so. In retrospect, I imagine she's glad her father had our marriage annulled. She certainly took it well enough when it happened. He shipped her off to Hawaii and she never even wrote me a goodbye note."

"That's hard to believe." Stanley replied incredulously. "She seems like a very considerate young woman."

"I used to think she was. I found out differently."

"Did you? Hmm. That seems a bit oversimplified. Have you discussed the matter with her?"

"No."

"Why not?"

"There's no need," Shaun said firmly. "Delia has her life and I have mine. Any chances we may have had in the past are long gone."

"You don't believe in second chances?"

"No."

"Too bad," Stanley said. "Too bad. If we hadn't had this little chat I'd have suspected the Blanchard money might be what was bothering you." He smiled wistfully. "There was a time when I'd have given almost anything to have had the bankroll Ronald was born with. Now that I'm older and wiser I can see that the Good Lord knew exactly what He was doing. I have my Eleanor and we're happy together in spite of everything. Ronald has nothing but his fat wallet and a lot of problems."

Shaun snorted derisively. "Only a man with enough money to do as he pleases feels that way."

"Oh, I don't know. Shakespeare says it best in *Henry the Eighth.*

I swear, 'tis better to be lowly born,
And range with humble livers in content,
Than to be perked up in a glistening grief,
And wear a golden sorrow.

Stanley paused in his recitation and smiled at Shaun. "Or, as the Bible says in Proverbs, 'Better is a dinner of herbs where love is, than a fattened ox and hatred therewith.'"

"Your family members have meaningful quotes for every occasion, don't they?" Shaun said, returning the older man's grin.

"The wisdom of the ages is always apropos." He grew more solemn and stepped away. "Well, I'd better be getting back to Eleanor before she starts to worry. Will we see you there tonight?"

"Yes. Delia asked me to come, too."

Stanley's smile returned. "Did she? Well, well. Can't say that I'm surprised."

"I'm just going as a friend, to back her up in case she needs it."

"Friendship is the best way to start," Stanley said. "If I were to believe the social pundits of today, I'd think good marriages only came about after a couple had played house and mucked around for who-knows-how-long. In my humble opinion, you can't build a better foundation for a life together than a strong, stable friendship. You mark my words, son."

Shaun bid him goodbye and watched him walk away. It was strange how much he liked the older man. Maybe Stanley reminded him of his own father, although he couldn't imagine how. On the surface the two men were very different. Yet there was an undercurrent of shared Christian beliefs and moral fiber, wasn't there? Perhaps that was the commonality. Both men had faced adversity and loss and had come through with their faith not only intact but strengthened.

For that, Shaun envied them. Maybe having faith was like having money. If Shaun had a lot, he didn't worry about getting more, and if he had very little, he was always seeking an increase. He supposed that could be true. Then again, who was he to speculate on the finer points of faith when his was so lacking?

What would it take to fix his spiritual deficiency? he wondered. How could he renew himself without relinquishing his character, his self-made strength? That was what had kept him together when he'd lost Delia, and again when he'd stood at attention as they laid his army buddies to rest with a twenty-one-gun salute. If he released his tight hold on himself, assuming he actually could, what would he have left?

Shaun set his jaw and headed for his truck. He wasn't about to let go of anything and take the chance that God would decide to pick up the pieces.

He'd come this far under his own steam and he was going to finish that way. Period.

FOURTEEN

Delia couldn't remember ever being this nervous in her whole life. She had picked at her supper while hoping that no one would notice her lack of appetite, especially her father.

Miranda, aware of the coming conflict, had shaken so badly throughout the meal her tremors would have jiggled the table had it not been so substantially built. And Winnie wasn't faring much better.

Wisely, Juliet had made the excuse that she was dining in town with Brandon and Portia and had promised to arrive in time for dessert.

That left only Shaun and the Halls unaccounted for. For her own sake, Delia dearly wished she'd made more precise arrangements but it was too late now.

Ronald sipped the last of his coffee, placed his linen napkin beside his plate and started to rise. "Well…"

Delia ordered, "No. Wait," so loudly that everyone startled, including her father.

He scowled at her. "What is the matter with you, Delia? You've been jumpy as a cat tonight."

"I have good reason to be," she said. "Please, let Sonya clear the table if you want, but don't leave. I need to talk to you."

"So, talk." He shrugged his shoulders beneath his expensive suit coat and straightened his silk tie. "I don't have all night."

"Excuse me just a minute," she said. "I think I hear the buzzer. I need to go open the gate. At least I think I do." *And if not, I'll phone the others and tell them all to hurry,* she added to herself. *Before this suspense kills me.*

To her relief, Shaun was the one ringing for admittance. She released the gates, then opened the heavy front door to wait on the porch, delighted to find her maternal grandparents arriving at the same time.

Shaun parked and took the steps two at a time.

Delia broke into a wide grin and murmured, "Thank you, Jesus," before she raised her voice to call, "Everybody come on in. It's time to get started."

The moment Shaun reached her he tenderly touched her arm. "Are your sisters here?"

"Not all of them. Juliet and Portia are late. Father's getting restless so I'm going to start without them."

"Okay. After you." He stood aside so Eleanor and Stanley could pass, then followed them and Delia into the dining room.

Ronald got to his feet and scowled. "What is this, some kind of a surprise party?"

"Not exactly, Father," Delia said. "I did invite some people but this is no party. I have something to ask you and I thought it was only fair for the Halls to be here, too."

"Ask me? Ask me what? What are you talking about?" he turned his frigid gaze on Shaun. "You'd better not have had anything to do with this, Murphy."

"Leave Shaun out of it, Father. He's just here as a friend. You're the one who involved him in the first place. Remember?"

"I just wanted somebody to look after you," Ronald insisted. "I didn't intend to make him a part of the family any more than Sonya or Andre or Peg are. They work for us. That's all."

Embarrassed, Delia rested her gaze on Shaun long enough to be sure he was going to hold his temper. His jaw was clenched but he nodded to her, clearly understanding her unspoken concern.

Fingers trembling, Delia reached into the pocket of the designer jeans Juliet had given her and withdrew a folded sheet of paper. Without explanation, she handed it to her father.

He looked annoyed at first. Then, his countenance darkened as he read what was printed. "Where did you get this?"

"That doesn't matter," Delia said. "What we want is an explanation. What do you know about Cymbeline Corporation?"

"Why?"

"You know why." Her voice was rising to match

her ire. "That was where the money came from that financed Mother's illegal hospitalization all those years."

"So?"

"So? *So?*" Delia was practically shouting. Shaun stepped to her side as she continued, "So, just how much did you know about what Aunt Genie was doing?"

"I simply gave her money to look after your mother," Ronald said stiffly.

"Yes, but she was the one who okayed the debits to the Cymbeline account and you were the one who kept it solvent, so you must have known everything. *Everything,* including exactly where and how that money was being spent."

"No, I…" Ronald looked as if he'd planned to argue more. Then, he sank back into his chair, rested his elbows on the table and put his face in his hands, the fight suddenly gone out of him. "That's not how it was."

"Then how was it? Tell us."

When he looked up, there were unshed tears in his eyes. The sight of her father showing any emotion other than anger or self-righteousness took Delia aback.

"I did set up Cymbeline," he admitted. "Years ago. It was Genie's idea to do it that way. She was supposed to look after your mother, to keep her from ever coming back to bother us after she signed away her parental rights. I just never dreamed…"

Winnie leaned forward and pointed a long,

tapering finger at her brother. "You can't possibly expect us to believe that fairy tale, Ronald. You were always very thorough. Very competent. You never did anything halfway. Nor did you leave important details to underlings. You knew where Trudy was. You had to."

Ronald was shaking his head emphatically. "No. No, I didn't. I swear it. Genie lied to me. She told me she was taking good care of Trudy. Why shouldn't I have trusted her? She was Trudy's sister!"

"What happened after Mother escaped from Westside Medical Retreat?" Delia asked, listening to her own heart thudding while Eleanor sobbed softly in the background.

"Genie came back here and got in touch with me," Ronald explained. "We agreed to meet in the gazebo. I thought we were going to discuss what had happened but she threatened me instead. She said she had Trudy put away somewhere safe and she wanted a lot more money or she'd go to the police and tell them I was guilty of false imprisonment and spousal abuse."

"Did you pay her off?"

"No! I refused to give her one cent more until I'd seen Trudy for myself and made sure she was alive and well."

Delia could hardly breathe. "Did Genie agree to let you see her?"

"No." He shook his head sadly. "She wouldn't listen to reason. She threatened to tell you, to tell all of you, to blame *me* for what she'd done. She said she had no qualms about blackmailing me if that was what it took to get me to keep adding more money to the Cymbeline account."

Shaun lightly touched Delia's arm in a show of unspoken support. She glanced at him before she ventured, "You solved the problem by killing Genie, didn't you, Father?"

"Of course not." Ronald's jaw went slack. He looked incredulous. "What kind of man do you think I am?"

"Never mind what I think. The facts are right there for everybody to see," Delia said tonelessly. "You knew about Mother all along and you told lie after lie to keep her from us. You dealt with Genie for years and then denied being acquainted with her at all until you were forced to admit collusion. By your own admission you fought with her in the gazebo right before she died, then you acted confused when we found her body in the library."

Delia paused and swallowed past the lump in her throat. "You say she threatened to expose you. Is that why you shot her, Father? Or was it because you didn't want to have to continue to pay her?"

"Neither." Tears were rolling down Ronald's face and his distinguished persona had vanished. "I didn't shoot anyone. I swear I didn't!"

Delia wasn't quite finished. She stood tall and spoke boldly. "The worst thing you did was to keep lying and lead everyone to believe that Mother was the victim. How could you let us continue to think we were burying our mother? How dare you?"

"I *did* think Genie was Trudy," Ronald insisted. "I hadn't seen either of them face-to-face for years, except that night in the gazebo when I confronted Genie. It was dark when we met and she kept her back to the porch light so I didn't get a good look at her.

"When we heard the ruckus in the library and found the body there, I immediately recognized the silk scarf I'd bought your mother on our trip to Italy. I was positive she had to be the one wearing it." His voice broke. "I—I thought Genie had brought Trudy into the house and shot her there just to get even with me."

"What about after the fact, when we got the DNA results back? What then?"

"By then I had decided Genie must have broken into the house intending to rob me. We have valuable paintings, expensive vases, jewelry. She wanted money and I wouldn't give it to her so I figured she'd decided to steal some things and sell them, instead."

From the doorway leading to the entryway, a man's voice asked, "What did you do with the gun, Mr. Blanchard?"

Delia's head snapped around. Her father leaped to his feet and gaped. Not only had Juliet and Brandon arrived, Portia had brought Detective Mick Campbell, her fiancé. It was Mick who had spoken.

"That was the only piece of the puzzle we couldn't find," Mick continued. "It'll go easier on you if you come clean."

"I don't know anything about a gun," Ronald bellowed.

Mick had left the others and approached the dining table. He stood facing Ronald and began to read him his rights. "Ronald Blanchard. You're under arrest for the murder of Genie Hall. You have the right to remain silent. If you give up this right…"

Over the hammering of her heart and her rapid, uneven breathing, Delia barely heard what was being said. She supposed she'd known, at least subconsciously, that her accusations could lead to this, yet she hadn't wanted to actually see it happen. No matter what the man had or hadn't done, he was still her father.

Her thoughts and regrets weren't rational, she knew, but she couldn't help blaming herself for what was taking place. Father was going to jail for murder, a murder he might very well have committed, and she had brought about his downfall.

Instead of rejoicing, she felt ashamed. Ashamed of her father for all his backstabbing and double-dealing, and ashamed of herself for being his daughter.

Delia knew she should be glad to have solved at least part of the mystery but right now, all she wanted to do was run and hide like the frightened little girl she'd been on that stormy night when her mother had first disappeared.

She felt Shaun's arm encircle her shoulders and she stiffened. He must be glad to see the arrest, too, after all her father had done to him. To them. She'd thought that bringing about justice would make her feel good, give her relief, joy, peace. It did none of those things.

On the contrary, she felt worse than ever.

* * *

I'll kill *her!*

The eavesdropper's fury built until there was no room for rational thought. *I should have gotten rid of her before this, before she stuck around too long and ruined everything.*

Think! Think! What now? There's no way I can stop what's happening but there must be something I can do to take charge of the situation.

Murderous thoughts whirled, tumbled, threatened to bring actions that would reveal far too much.

Breathe deeply, get a grip on yourself and don't let anyone see how upset you are. There's nothing that can be done now. Nothing. Bide your time. Be patient. Your opportunity will come. And then Delia Blanchard won't be a problem for anyone ever again because her life will be over.

The listener smiled. *It will have to be an accident of some kind. Perhaps something to do with that rental car. Or, maybe, an overdose like the one that had almost taken care of crazy old Howard. And the sooner the better.*

It was late in the evening before the sisters unwound enough to call it a night. Delia had bidden goodbye to the Halls shortly after Ronald's arrest. Portia and Juliet had lingered outside in Brandon's car, talking with him for hours, while Winnie had gone to bed with polite apologies. Only Shaun had stayed behind with Delia and he, too, had finally decided to head home.

She walked him to the door and out onto the wide, stone porch. It was amazing how awkward they had all acted once Mick had led Ronald off in handcuffs. Nobody had seemed to know what to say. Those who had tried to carry on a normal conversation had come across as either too somber or inanely superficial.

Shaun paused in the dimness of the porch light to grasp her fingers and hold them while his thumbs caressed the backs of her hands. "Will you be okay?"

She huffed. "I doubt I'll ever be okay again. This is unbelievable. My own father."

"I never did like him much but I kind of felt sorry for him tonight," Shaun said. "He was a broken man."

"He'll recover. He always does. It's a trait he inherited from his father."

"Speaking of Howard," Shaun said while glancing up at the third floor where the old man's suite was, "how is he doing these days?"

"Better. The doctors credit Peg with keeping him going. She's a very devoted nurse. We're fortunate to have her."

"What about the potassium poisoning that put him in the hospital? Any clues to how it came about?"

Delia chewed on her lower lip and shook her head. "No. Though I wouldn't be surprised to see Father suspected of doing that, too. He had means, motive and opportunity. Plus, he stands to inherit an obscene amount of money when Grandfather is out of the picture."

"Do *you* think he did it?"

"I don't know what to think. If you had asked me a month ago how I felt about my father, I'd have told you that I thought he was a stern taskmaster but not an evil man. Now, who knows? He might be guilty of even more heinous crimes than we've uncovered so far." She sighed. "Whatever he has or hasn't done, I don't intend to stick around and watch the police work on it."

"You're going back to Hawaii soon?"

"Yes."

"I can understand that. I'll be leaving soon, too, I hope. I've had a long talk with Dad and convinced him it's time for him to sell the woodworking business and retire. As soon as we can make a deal that's fair, I'll hit the road."

She pulled her hands free of his grasp. "That's good to hear. About Ian retiring, I mean. I had hoped to see you once in a while when I came back to visit. Guess that's not going to happen, huh?"

"It's just as well," Shaun said gruffly. "We have to get on with our lives."

"I suppose so. I should have asked. Do you have someone special waiting for you somewhere?"

"No. Not anymore." His gaze darkened and he stuffed his hands into the pockets of his jacket. "Well, if I don't see you again before you go, have a great life, Dee."

He'd used her pet name again. That gave her hope. "Thanks. You, too." Hesitating, gathering her courage, she decided there would never be a better time to speak honestly. If she let this moment pass she knew she'd regret it forever. "Is it too late for us?" she asked softly.

He set his jaw and nodded.

"Okay. I had to ask. I...thanks for everything, Shaun. I couldn't have managed without you."

"Yes, you could. But you're welcome. If you ever need a friend..."

"I'll know just where to come," she finished for him, even though they both knew it wasn't so. Wherever he decided to go, he wasn't planning on leaving a forwarding address so she could track him down.

Taking a step back, Delia noted that he did the same. "Good night, Shaun."

"Bye, Delia."

She wanted to stand there and watch him until he got back in his truck and drove out of sight but she knew better than to chance it. The only way to hide the raw emotions that were threatening to erupt was to turn and duck back into the house.

Closing the heavy front door, she leaned against the inside of it and held her breath until she heard the sound of Shaun's truck fade away.

This promised to be a long, sleepless night, the first of many to come, she reasoned, fighting tears and swiping them off her cheeks in disgust.

Well, there was no use delaying the inevitable. She was sick of weeping. Sick of being miserable. Sick of facing the impossibility of ever getting back together with the man she loved. The most sensible course was exactly what she had just told Shaun she planned to do. Come morning she was going to book a flight to Oahu and go back to where she truly belonged. If peace and contentment were to be found anywhere, she'd find them in Hawaii.

Padding upstairs to the guest room, Delia found a lovely plate of perfectly made petit fours waiting on her nightstand. There was no note with them but she assumed that either Winnie or one of her sisters, knowing she was upset, had left them for her.

She picked one up, started to take a bite, then stopped. Shaun was right. Trying to eat her cares away was a foolhardy method of dealing with adversity. No amount of chocolate would make her happy or solve her problems. Only prayer and trusting the Lord could do that.

Still, the sweet treat did smell wonderful. Maybe just one little bite…

No. One bite would lead to another and another until the whole plate of desserts was gone. As much as she appreciated the kindness of whoever had left the petit fours, she wasn't going to give in to temptation.

Out of sight, out of mind, Delia thought, carrying the plate to the door of her room and placing it outside in the hallway on the floor.

"There. That's better," she told herself with pride at the sensible choice. Making her way to the bed she paused, then knelt and closed her eyes.

Her ensuing prayer was more tears than astute words and phrases but Delia didn't care. She knew that even though she didn't understand why things had worked out the way they had, God was still in control. Her most fervent wish was for the ability to trust Him in all things and at all times, instead of only when her life was going smoothly.

It had been especially difficult saying goodbye to Aunt Winnie the next morning. Miranda had understood why Delia wanted to leave Stoneley, as had her other sisters. After all, most of them were in the process of breaking away and making new lives for themselves and they wanted the best for her, too.

It looked as if Brandon was going to wind up at the helm of Blanchard Fabrics, at least for the present, and that meant Juliet would also stick around, but that was a temporary solution at best.

Barbara Sanchez, Ronald's executive assistant, would help during the transition, of course, but if he was granted bail he'd undoubtedly want to go back to work. What would eventually become of the company if—when—he was convicted of Genie's murder was anybody's guess.

Delia closed her eyes and leaned the airliner seat back to try to rest. The long flight across the Mainland and out over the Pacific had given her plenty of time to think, which wasn't necessarily a good thing.

In calm retrospect, however, she could see details of the night her father had been arrested with much more clarity and she'd relived those events over and over until she was totally worn-out.

Even the servants, who were used to the normally

tense atmosphere in Blanchard manor, had behaved strangely that evening. When Sonya had cleared the table she'd watched everyone out of the corners of her eyes as if expecting bizarre behavior or even danger. And when Peg had come downstairs to get a dish of pudding for Grandfather Howard's bedtime snack she'd seemed so distracted, so worried, she'd hardly spoken to anyone.

Poor Miranda was taking things the hardest, Delia concluded. As the eldest, she had known their mother best and remembered more about her so the added trauma and lack of answers would naturally affect her deeply. In Miranda's case, however, it seemed to be worse than anyone had expected. Not only was she close to becoming a recluse, she'd begun to believe she was hearing plaintive music where there was only silence and she had actually started humming along! If Miranda hadn't had Aunt Winnie and Juliet for companionship, Delia might have considered delaying her departure just to give her sister more emotional support.

The plane banked to Delia's side as it approached Honolulu International Airport. Below, the crystal clear water near the shoreline shimmered in shades of turquoise and azure, delineated here and there by breaking waves. Farther out, she could see white sails dotted against the darker depths like kites in a clear summer sky.

Motor launches were less noticeable but they left curving wakes that reminded her of the arching branches of the bougainvillea that spread riotous color over the west-facing wall of her beachfront home near Ehukai.

The pilot leveled off and began his descent for landing. The skyscrapers of Honolulu rose to Delia's right and in the distance she could see Pearl Harbor and the memorial to the USS *Arizona*. To her left was the part of the island she loved best, the undeveloped sea of green that represented Oahu the way it once was.

She sighed with relief. *Home*. She was home. Finally. Although her heart was gladdened to have arrived, there was still a stone in the midst of it, keeping her from realizing the full-fledged joy that usually accompanied her arrival in the Islands.

"Well, that can't be helped," she told herself as she deplaned, lugging her carry-on bag.

She began to smile as she reached the concourse and saw all the wide grins and leis awaiting her fellow passengers. Although the traditional floral garlands weren't often given to tourists before they reached their hotels, locals still greeted friends and family the traditional way—with warmth, embraces and a necklace of delicate, fragrant blooms.

"I love this place," Delia murmured, passing through the crowd.

"You are kamaaina?" a nearby old woman asked pleasantly.

Delia returned her grin. "No. I wasn't born here. But it's my home, now."

"Then you should have this," the woman said, lifting

a graceful lavender-and-white garland over Delia's head with both hands and placing it around her neck.

Delia was touched and thanked her with a nod and a gentle smile. *"Mahalo."*

"You are welcome. No one is meeting you?"

"No. Not this time. I left my car here when I flew to the Mainland."

"Then aloha," the old woman said, flashing another grin that brightened her dark eyes and crinkled the leathered skin around them. "Ah! I think I see my daughter." She hesitated long enough to study Delia's expression, then added, *"Onipa'a,"* before she turned away and blended into the crowd.

Delia blinked, puzzled, and stared after her. What a strange thing to say. What could possibly have caused the old woman to quote Queen Liliuokalani's motto and warn her to *Take a stand and do right no matter what?*

Reminded of the rightness of her recent confrontation with her father, Delia took the woman's comment as welcome confirmation, smiling as she headed outside to the causeway that led to the baggage claim area.

All her cares were quickly forgotten when she was bathed in the warm, humid Hawaiian air. After the air-conditioning in the plane and the terminal, the freshness of the outdoors was a most welcome change.

Delia breathed deeply of the freedom, the sweetness that was so much a part of the Islands. Every time she returned she had the same reaction, the same feeling of euphoria and peace.

This time, however, something was missing. She didn't have to do much soul-searching to decide what the missing element was. Part of her heart and soul had remained behind in Maine. The part she had given to Shaun.

It made no difference that he had chosen to reject her gift of love. It still belonged to him. There was nothing she could do to change that.

And, searching her innermost thoughts for the truth, she realized that that was exactly the way she wanted it.

She's gone. She escaped. I can't believe she turned down the sweets. She never does that. She loves chocolate! And because I thought the problem was solved I didn't take the time to sabotage her car.

Muttered curses filled the air. *After all she's done she doesn't deserve to live. But what can I do now? I have to stay here. I have no choice. If I'd had one more day, maybe two, I could have dealt with her properly, have evened the score. But, no. She had to run off to Hawaii!*

Pacing, the plotter took care to keep from making too much noise. It would be nice to be able to shout, to throw things, to take aggression out on the surroundings. That wouldn't do, of course. There were images to preserve, personas to maintain at all costs. Their importance went beyond any individual desires.

Soon, it will be over. Soon, I'll be done with all of this. Then they'll all know the truth and they can thank me. It took a lot of courage to do what I've done so far. Courage and brains. But love will win out. It must. I'll see to it.

FIFTEEN

Shaun was restless and perplexed beyond anything he'd ever experienced. He'd tried to hide his feelings from his father but Ian wasn't fooled.

"What's the matter with you, son? You act like a man who's lost his best friend."

"I don't have best friends," Shaun countered, busying himself by sweeping wood scraps and shavings into a pile on the floor of the workroom. "Not since my stint in the army."

Ian chortled. "Oh, yeah? You could have fooled me. The way you'd been spending all your spare time with Delia, I was sure you and she had taken up where you left off." He paused long enough to laugh again. "What happened? Did she turn you down?"

"No." Shaun was scowling.

"Then why the long face?"

"It's complicated."

"I imagine so. Love usually is. 'Course, that's if you don't have a good woman like your mom was.

Seems to me you did have one, once. What went wrong?"

Shaun's frown deepened. He grabbed a chunk of scrap wood the size of his palm and threw it across the shed as if it were a baseball. It hit the corrugated wall with a tinny clang and bounced off. "You know exactly what went wrong. You lived through it with me. Ronald Blanchard waved his big fat checkbook and Delia trotted home like a puppy chasing a bone."

"She told you that, did she?"

"She didn't have to. I was there, remember?"

"Yup. So you said. I just wondered if you two had managed to talk about it lately. You know, rehash it and get all the details straight?"

"Why would I want to put myself through that again?"

Ian shrugged. He'd picked up a tapering scrap of basswood and was whittling at it with a pocketknife while he spoke. "Don't know. Maybe to see if there'd been a misunderstanding?"

"You think I'm wrong? Is that what you're trying to say?"

"I thought that's what I *was* sayin'." Ian laughed again, more quietly this time. "You and that girl have been running all over tarnation, supposedly looking for the truth, yet you never bothered to look inside your own hearts. What kind of fool does that?"

"This kind," Shaun grumbled. "So, you think I've blown my chances?"

"Not necessarily." The older man whittled some more. "You ever have the urge to see Hawaii, son?"

"I can't go chasing her halfway around the world."

"Okay. Suit yourself. If this was about your mother and me, I'd already be on that plane."

"That's different. You loved Mom."

Ian lowered the chunk of wood and his pocketknife and stared at Shaun. "Okay. Tell me you don't have any loving feelings for Delia Blanchard and I'll shut up." He paused for a few seconds, then burst into laughter when Shaun didn't deny it. "Hah! Thought so. Well, what're you waiting for?"

"I can't leave Stoneley. You need me."

"I've done okay for the past ten or twelve years. I think I can manage to sell this place by myself," Ian said. "Already got a couple of prospective buyers. Besides, if you're right and Delia isn't the woman I think she is, you won't be gone long."

"What makes you think I'm the right man for her?" Shaun asked pensively.

"Suppose we let her decide that."

"I'll think about it," Shaun said. "But I'm not promising anything."

Ian shrugged. "Suits me. If I were you, I'd do a bit of prayin', too. Can't hurt. Might help."

Touched, Shaun hid behind humor to protect himself from deeper feelings. "I tried it once. It didn't do me any good."

"That's probably because you treated your prayers like you were givin' God a grocery list and expecting Him to fill it." Ian was slowly shaking his head. "I learned the hard way that it doesn't work like that. If it did, I'd of had a lot more years with your mother."

He managed a smile as he gazed lovingly at his only son. "Besides, you can't order from the store if you don't have an account there. Why should the Good Lord listen to you if you don't claim to be one of His children?"

"More Murphy wisdom?" Shaun said. "It's getting pretty deep in here, Dad."

"Just think about it. That's all I ask. If you wait till you're as old and set in your ways as I was before you let God into your life, you're liable to miss out on a lot of blessings."

Like being married to Delia? Shaun added to himself. *Was there really a chance for them?*

He supposed there was only one way to find out. He'd have to swallow his stupid pride, forgive her for whatever she may have done in the past, and go ask her, point-blank.

Humph. Well, it couldn't be any harder than walking barefoot over hot coals. Shaun smiled. That silly thought had reminded him of the way Delia had danced across the ruined sofa in her Aunt Genie's apartment when they'd fought with Erik Evans.

He sobered. He had prayed then, too, hadn't he? It wasn't the formal, religious kind of prayer he'd heard in church, it was the kind that came from the gut, from the soul.

The truth hit him like a ton of bricks. He *did* believe. He always had, even when he'd gone out of his way to deny his faith rather than admit that there were many things about life's journey that he didn't even begin to understand.

Father, forgive me, came directly from his heart and settled in his whirling mind. He wasn't in this alone. He had divine help. All he had to do was access it. Trust it.

One thing Shaun knew for a fact. Delia was in Hawaii and he needed to talk to her, face-to-face, not on the telephone.

He wanted to see her expression, to look into her beautiful dark eyes when he told her he loved her and he wanted them to try again. If she laughed or rejected him, so be it. Nothing could be worse than the agony of wondering that he was experiencing right now.

It took Delia several days to catch up on the backlog of paperwork and unanswered calls her teenage assistant had left piled on her desk. Lily was a dear but she was not the most organized person in the world. Delia doubted the girl would have been able to find the Pacific Ocean if it hadn't been located practically right outside their back door.

She had finally gotten tired of listening to the girl's lame excuses and had sent her to Sunset Beach that afternoon to watch her latest boyfriend surf. The lanky teen had come to Delia for lessons and he did show promise but his infatuation with Lily had definitely been a distraction.

"I am not jealous," Delia told herself, making her way down the center aisle of the surf shop to lock up for the day.

The denial echoed in the empty store, bouncing off the racks of wet suits, flippers, masks and carefully stacked fiberglass boards.

Yes, you are, her traitorous conscience countered. *You're lonesome and miserable and as jealous as you can be.*

"Can't very well win an argument when I take both sides, can I?" Delia grumbled.

Well, so what if she was miserable. She'd had her heart broken before and it hadn't killed her, even though she'd thought sure it would. She'd get over it this time, too.

But, oh, how she missed Shaun. Every waking moment was filled with memories of their recent time together and there was no peace to be had in slumber, either. He was a part of all her dreams, awake or asleep.

His smile had warmed her like the tropical sun on her face, his gentle touch reminding her of the heated sand shifting beneath her toes, caressing the soles of her bare feet. Like it or not, memories of Shaun were as much a part of her as breathing.

Delia flipped the open sign to Closed, slammed the door and reached for the tab on the dead bolt as she gazed out the window without focusing on anything in particular.

Suddenly her hand stilled. Her breath caught. Her heart began to race. There was a man approaching whose walk seemed awfully familiar. His hair was dark and his eyes were shaded by sunglasses but there was something about him that caught and held her attention.

Wishful thinking, she told herself. *You want to see Shaun so you're imagining him everywhere. You thought you saw him in the grocery store yesterday, remember? And what about the guy you chased down the boardwalk just because he was wearing a red ball cap like the one Shaun bought at the zoo? Get a grip, girl!*

Delia stood very still and stared. The stranger seemed to be headed straight for her shop. Hands trembling, she reversed the dead bolt and opened the door.

The man saw her and began to smile.

Delia blinked in disbelief. It really *was* Shaun. And he was coming closer by the second!

He'd never seen a more beautiful sight in his life. Delia was standing in the doorway as if she'd been waiting for him all along. Thank God, literally, that she hadn't closed the store before he'd managed to find it. If he'd had to wait till the following morning to see her, to talk to her, he'd have been a nervous wreck.

Removing his sunglasses Shaun quickly closed the distance between them. She did seem happy to see him, which was a definite relief. He wanted to sweep her into his arms and swing her around the way he used to when they were younger but he was afraid to overstep and frighten her off before he knew exactly where their relationship stood.

"Shaun? Shaun! It *is* you. I thought I was imagining things."

"Hello, Dee." She didn't slam the door in his face

or run, so he figured he must be on pretty firm ground. "Are you surprised?"

"Astonished. What are you doing here?"

"I had some unfinished business to take care of," he said, stepping closer and lowering his voice.

"Business? What—what business?"

Gently, slowly, he cupped her cheeks with his palms, then bent to kiss her. Judging by the way she went kind of limp in his arms, he was doing well. So far. The tricky part was still to come. He'd rehearsed it and rehearsed it, changing his approach many times, and he had yet to be satisfied that whatever he said would be received in the loving way he meant it.

"Shaun?" Delia's palms had been pressed to his chest. Now, she pushed away just enough to gaze into his eyes.

"You were right," he said. "We should have talked about what happened twelve years ago. But you know what? I've decided it doesn't matter. I don't care about all that."

"You don't?"

"No. We don't have to be victims of our past mistakes."

She gave him a harder push. "Whoa. Wait a minute, buster. Are you saying marrying me was a mistake?"

Uh-oh. "No. I didn't mean anything like that. I just want you to know I forgive you."

Delia's eyes widened. "Forgive me? For *what?*"

"For running off on our wedding night."

"I didn't run off. You did."

Shaun frowned at her. "What are you talking about? I went out to get you the ice cream you'd asked for and when I came back, you were gone." He could see the warring emotions in her expression. Finally, she stopped resisting his embrace and relaxed so he continued, "The hotel room was empty and all your things were gone, Dee. What was I supposed to think?"

"Father said…" Tears filled her eyes and began to slide quietly down her cheeks. "He said he'd paid you off. That's why you left. And I believed him, so I went along with the annulment."

"I tried over and over to see you. To talk to you. Your father insisted that you didn't want anything more to do with me. When I learned you'd moved all the way to Hawaii, I finally gave up."

"Oh, Shaun. If only we'd believed in each other more."

His jaw clenched. "It wasn't all our fault, Dee. We had plenty of help messing up our lives."

"My father has a lot to atone for."

"Forget Ronald," Shaun said. "All that matters is you and me. I've never stopped loving you, Delia."

Tears filled her eyes. "Oh, Shaun. I love you, too. More than you'll ever know."

A grin spread across his face. "I was hoping you'd say that." He clasped her hand tightly. "Marry me, Delia? Marry me again? We'll get it right this time, I promise."

"When? Where?" Her eyes were bright, her smile wide.

244 **Deadly Payoff**

"Is that a yes?"

"Yes!"

She threw her arms around his neck and Shaun finally lifted her feet off the ground and twirled her in a circle the way he'd wanted to from the moment he'd seen her standing there.

"I don't want you to get away from me again," Shaun said, keeping his arms around her as he lowered her. "I know you probably want to go back to Maine so your sisters and Winnie can be part of our wedding but…"

"I know exactly how you feel," she said happily. "Come on. Let's walk along the beach and talk."

Now that he'd finally gotten his wife back, Shaun was loath to release her, even for a moment, so he grasped her hand as they began to stroll toward the shore.

"So, what do you want to do?" Shaun finally asked.

Delia giggled and blushed. "Well, I hate to sound too forward but it seems to me we're about twelve years late for our honeymoon. What do you say we get married here, in a simple ceremony, then repeat our vows later, maybe as part of one of my sisters' weddings?"

"That sounds great."

"We could get married on the beach," Delia suggested. "I'm sure Pastor Jim, from my church, would be glad to officiate if we can work around his schedule. People hold services outside all the time here."

"What about a license? Blood tests?"

"Hawaiians are a very laid-back group," she said, smiling broadly. "All you and I need to do is appear together before the marriage license agent, pay the fee and we get our license. It's easy. There's no waiting, no residence requirement, no complications."

Shaun pulled her closer. "So, there's nothing to stop us from making this official real soon?"

"Nothing at all," she said, "if you're sure about it. You've told me more than once that you're worried about my surfing. I'm not about to stop doing it, you know."

"I know. I'll adjust. I can't promise I won't lose sleep over it but I know how much your career means to you. I would never try to take that away from you."

"Thank you. And speaking of careers, what about Ian? Doesn't he need you back in Maine?"

Shaun grinned. "Not according to him. He's planning to retire. Now that I've seen this place, I think the climate might do him good. Would you mind if he lived close by?"

"No! Not at all. That's a wonderful idea. You might even want to start building things here. We have some wonderful tropical woods available." She suddenly looked uncertain. "I don't mean to be pushy. I mean, I wouldn't want you to rush into anything if you're not ready."

"That's not a problem," Shaun said, cupping her cheeks with his hands and gazing upon her with a depth of tenderness and love far beyond anything he'd thought he'd possessed. "Like you said, we're about twelve years late beginning our honeymoon. I think I'm more than ready."

"Yes," she replied with a telling smile. "So, am I."

They stood together on the warm shore, hands joined, beneath a flower-bedecked arch of palm fronds. The ocean was calm, the heavens cloudless. As the tide receded it left behind scalloped bands of froth that edged the gentle waves like lace on a traditional wedding gown.

Delia wore a sarong of softly draped Hawaiian print fabric in muted shades that echoed the sea and sky. She had bought Shaun a matching shirt and white slacks. Instead of the traditional bride's bouquet she had tucked orchids in her hair and placed three leis around her neck.

The pastor was also dressed casually, mostly in white, and his burnished face glowed with a spiritual aura and pure delight as he pronounced them man and wife.

He raised a hand in benediction. "*I ho'okahi kahi ke aloha.* Be one in love."

Delia's eyes filled with happy tears. The first time she and Shaun had taken their marriage vows they had done so in defiance of her father. This time, they were free to promise unending love without it being a result of lies and deceit. In contrast, the immense peace that filled her this time was truly amazing.

She had spoken with her sisters and Shaun had called Ian prior to the ceremony so everyone would know what was happening. Delia's Hawaiian friends were arranged in a semicircle around them on the beach holding borrowed cell phones that transmitted live video. One was sending pictures to the Blanchard estate for Miranda, Winnie and Juliet, one was sending images to Bianca in Boston, one was connected to Rissa in New York, one was going to the Coastal Inn for the Halls, and the last was Portia's. She had volunteered to take her phone to Ian's after she closed her shop so he could also be included. Thanks to the differences in time zones, the wedding could take place in the afternoon in Hawaii and their families could watch it in the evening on the east coast of the Mainland.

"You may kiss the bride," Pastor Jim said, grinning.

"About time," Shaun whispered as he bent to oblige.

Delia agreed wholeheartedly. She slipped her arms around his neck and stood on tiptoe to return his kiss.

In the background, the crowd of well-wishers, which included both friends and passing tourists, cheered.

She and Shaun turned, still half embracing, and waved to their families via the cell phones.

"I'm sorry you couldn't have been here with us," Delia announced loudly, "but you've seen everything and I promise we'll do this again later, just for you." She blew them a kiss. "Bye now. Aloha!"

She gazed up at her new husband through a mist of pure joy as their guests ended the telephone transmissions.

"You don't fool me," Shaun said quietly aside.

Delia gave him a mock scowl. "About what?"

"Your lame excuses for wanting to get married so far from Stoneley. I know exactly what you're doing."

"You do?"

"Uh-huh. There's cake involved in this wedding and you want it all for yourself."

Delia hugged him as she laughed. "You think you know me so well, don't you? Well, believe me, husband, that isn't *all* I want for myself."

His eyebrow arched. "Oh? Would you care to explain?"

"Later," she said, still giggling. "First, we need to go cut that cake you mentioned. I'm suddenly famished."

"Are you changing the subject, Dee?"

"Yes!" Cheeks flaming, she ducked her head, took his hand and tugged him toward the picnic table where their guests—and the first minutes of their future as a married couple—awaited them.

* * * * *

Is Ronald Blanchard truly guilty of murder?
Can Miranda Blanchard shed the fears
that bind her…and find love?
Find out in WHERE TRUTH LIES,
the exciting conclusion to
THE SECRETS OF STONELEY
coming from Love Inspired Suspense
in June 2007.

Dear Reader,

Once again I have been asked to collaborate with five other authors to create my part of an ongoing saga, which, in this case, is book five in the suspenseful SECRETS OF STONELEY miniseries.

Many thanks to my fellow authors, Lenora Worth, Shirlee McCoy, Terri Reed, Irene Brand and Lynn Bulock, and to our editor, Diane Dietz. We worked hard to make our series books fit together, as well as be stand-alone tales of love and faith overcoming mystery and danger. Thanks also to Jeannie O., who helped me get to know Hawaii.

In *Deadly Payoff,* Delia and Shaun get a second chance. I think it's important to remember that we are seldom given that precise a choice. Life isn't static and predictable like the chapters in a novel. We can't go back to the beginning or thumb through the pages until we get to a part we like and then relive it until we get it right. When we make mistakes we have to deal with the consequences and go on. Doing that successfully, under our own power, is next to impossible. Starting over with God's guidance is another story. No problem is so big, no mistake so bad that God can't help us. The key is not within ourselves, it's in our willingness to look to Him, to ask His forgiveness and to trust Him to bring us through, one step at a time.

I love to hear from readers. The quickest replies are by e-mail: valw@centurytel.net. Or you can write to me at P.O. Box 13, Glencoe, AR, 72539 and I'll do my best to answer as soon as I can. Or go to www.ValerieHansen.com

Blessings,

Valerie Hansen

QUESTIONS FOR DISCUSSION

1. This series deals with a big family. Do you come from such a family? If not, do you ever think you might like more siblings?

2. The Blanchard sisters each cope with past trauma in different ways. Does Delia's escape to Hawaii seem like a good solution? Why or why not?

3. Delia and Shaun are given what looks to us like a second chance, yet they're both hesitant to accept it. Have you ever been in a similar situation and let a chance for reconciliation slip away?

4. The Blanchards have a lot of money. Do you think they would be happier if their hearts were focused on giving, rather than on hoarding? Is money the problem at all?

5. Unseen forces seem to be working against the Blanchard family. Do you think the sins of the previous generation are responsible? Is there any escape for them?

6. Mental illness plays a big part in this series. Is this illness any different from other chronic illnesses? Should people be ostracized just because they're sick?

7. Delia realizes, belatedly, that her prayers for her mother have finally been answered. Have you ever thought back to your prayers of long ago and seen answers that you had previously overlooked?

8. Shaun turns away from God when he doesn't get the answers to his prayers that he expects. Why does it seem to be so hard for us to accept that God's wisdom is greater than our own? Do you often argue with Him?

9. Hebrews 11:1 says that "Faith is the substance [assurance] of things hoped for, the evidence [a conviction] of things not seen." How does remembering God's previous blessings help strengthen our daily faith?

10. If you could mete out divine justice for the characters in this series right now, what would you do? Who would you blame? Now that you've thought about that, aren't you glad our Heavenly Father forgives us much more readily than we are able to forgive each other?

REQUEST YOUR FREE BOOKS!
2 FREE RIVETING INSPIRATIONAL NOVELS
PLUS 2 FREE MYSTERY GIFTS

Love Inspired®
SUSPENSE

YES! Please send me 2 FREE Love Inspired® Suspense novels and my 2 FREE mystery gifts. After receiving them, if I don't wish to receive any more books, I can return the shipping statement marked "cancel." If I don't cancel, I will receive 4 brand-new novels every month and be billed just $3.99 per book in the U.S. or $4.74 per book in Canada, plus 25¢ shipping and handling per book and applicable taxes, if any*. That's a savings of 20% off the cover price! I understand that accepting the 2 free books and gifts places me under no obligation to buy anything. I can always return a shipment and cancel at any time. Even if I never buy another book from Steeple Hill, the two free books and gifts are mine to keep forever.

123 IDN EL5H 323 IDN ELQH

Name	(PLEASE PRINT)

Address	Apt. #

City	State/Prov.	Zip/Postal Code

Signature (if under 18, a parent or guardian must sign)

Order online at www.LoveInspiredSuspense.com

Or mail to Steeple Hill Reader Service™:

IN U.S.A.: P.O. Box 1867, Buffalo, NY 14240-1867
IN CANADA: P.O. Box 609, Fort Erie, Ontario L2A 5X3

Not valid to current Love Inspired Suspense subscribers.

Want to try two free books from another series?
Call 1-800-873-8635 or visit www.morefreebooks.com

* Terms and prices subject to change without notice. NY residents add applicable sales tax. Canadian residents will be charged applicable provincial taxes and GST. This offer is limited to one order per household. All orders subject to approval. Credit or debit balances in a customer's account(s) may be offset by any other outstanding balance owed by or to the customer. Please allow 4 to 6 weeks for delivery.

Your Privacy: Steeple Hill is committed to protecting your privacy. Our Privacy Policy is available online at www.eHarlequin.com or upon request from the Reader Service. From time to time we make our lists of customers available to reputable firms who may have a product or service of interest to you. If you would prefer we not share your name and address, please check here. ☐

LISUS07

Love Inspired SUSPENSE

TITLES AVAILABLE NEXT MONTH

Don't miss these four stories in June

GLORY BE! by Ron and Janet Benrey
Cozy mystery

An unexpected windfall had greedy church choir members preparing for a battle. Emma McCall wanted no part of it... until a VW Bug appeared on her porch. No one would take her complaint seriously—except the handsome deputy police chief.

WHERE TRUTH LIES by Lynn Bulock
The Secrets of Stoneley

Miranda Blanchard spent her life as a prisoner to her debilitating panic attacks. But Pastor Gregory Brown became a steadying force in her life as she and her sisters worked to unravel the mysteries that plague their family.

SHADOW OF TURNING by Valerie Hansen

Her Ozark hometown had always been a safe haven for Chancy Boyd. But now a series of crimes threatened her, and a deadly tornado—her worst nightmare—was racing toward the town. Only "storm chaser" Nate Collins could help her face her deepest fears.

CAUGHT IN A BIND by Gayle Roper

People don't vanish into thin air. Yet that's what happened to the husband of one of Merry Kramer's coworkers. And in his place? A strange corpse. Could Merry's search for the scoop spell doom for this spunky sleuth?

LISCNM0507